ASK ME SOMETHING EASY

NATALIE HONEYCUTT

AVON BOOKS
A division of
The Hearst Corporation
1350 Avenue of the Americas
New York, New York 10019

Published by arrangement with Orchard Books
Library of Congress Catalog Card Number: 90-7765
ISBN: 0-380-71723-9
RL: 4.9

First Avon Flare Printing: August 1993

AVON TRADEMARK REG. U.S. PAT. OFF. AND IN OTHER COUNTRIES, MARCA REGISTRADA, HECHO EN CANADA

Printed in Canada

UNV 10 9 8 7 6 5 4 3 2

For Bonnie and Nita,
the twins,
with love and lilacs

And for
Russell • Dick • Judy • Doug
whose gifts and blessings, fully felt,
may be found in here

One

Oh, Dinah, ask me something easy. Ask me what happens the day after forever. I've thought about that, and I have an answer waiting. Maybe you'd laugh if I told you, and that would be okay. I'd like to make you laugh again. It's been such a long time. . . .

But what happened to us? And who am I, really? Dinah, those questions are hard. *Harder yet for an almost seventeen-year-old tumbleweed.*

That's how I think of us. Tumbleweeds, all six—Mother, Daddy, you, me, and the twins. I keep thinking of how a tumbleweed starts out. Of how it's something else entirely—a sage-brush, say—until for some reason the sage dies and uproots. Then it blows about for a while, and as it does, its branches dry out and get bleached by the sun, and some are nicked right off from bouncing along over the desert ahead of the wind. Then, Dinah, when the used-to-be sage is all rounded and light as air, only then *is it a tumbleweed.*

If you asked me to choose a moment when our lives changed—when the wind shifted, driving in hard from the north, and picked us up and blew us off in a new direction—I guess I'd have to go back nearly ten years. To when you were ten and I was seven.

We lay in the dark in bed. It was a double bed, passed on to us by our parents, and my feet were twined through Dinah's. I was listening, or trying to listen, to Mama and Daddy argue downstairs. I don't know even now whether there was something special about that particular argument. It might have been longer than usual, or it might have been louder than usual, or it might have been just one argument too many. Whatever it was, I do know that Dinah was humming—a steady hum, strong—making it impossible for me to hear.

I nudged her in the side. "Hush," I said. "Quiet. I need to listen to this."

"Why?" Dinah asked. "What's the point? It's just the same old argument. They never have a new one. Do you really want to hear it again?"

"Yes," I said. I really did.

"Well, I don't," Dinah said.

Still, she didn't pick up humming, and in the quiet I tried with all my might to hear my parents. I wanted to make out words, but I couldn't. I could only hear voices. Or rather, my mother's voice. She would shout for a bit, then nothing, then she would shout some more. But I knew that in the spaces my father was arguing back. He just wasn't much of a shouter.

I wanted to hear so I'd know how the argument would end. If the fight was bad, it sometimes ended with Daddy stomping off into the night. And I wanted some warning this time. Just this once, when the door slammed, I meant to be ready.

Silence. Every so often a car drove past our house, and when it did, the beam from its headlights traveled around the room. The beam always traveled in the opposite direction from the car and I couldn't make sense of that. It went wavy when it ran across the rack where Dinah and I hung our dress-up hats and scarves, and I couldn't make sense of that either. But I could see in the passing light that Dinah's eyes were closed—not a restful kind of closed, but squinched—and her fingers were in her ears.

"Dinah?" I tugged on the sleeve of her nightie.

"Addie, *what?*"

"Do you think it's about money?" I asked.

"Of *course* it's about money," she said. "What else? He says she spends too much. She says he wastes it. She's a pennypincher and a nag, he's irresponsible and a dreamer. The Barbara and Lucas Dillon All-Purpose Fight."

Dinah was right. The arguments were so alike you could trade one for another and never notice the difference.

"What I don't get," I said to her, "is why. Why do they fight about money if we're rich? We are rich, aren't we?"

Dinah didn't answer.

"We must be rich," I decided. "We have to be. We have this big house that is almost brand-new. And all our furniture is new. Well, most of it, anyway. And we have a trash compactor and two cars."

"And two TVs," Dinah added.

"See?" I was nearly sure of it now. "And toys. Lots of toys. And a microwave oven and the twins."

Dinah laughed. "You can't count the twins," she said. "They didn't buy them, Addie, for pete's sake! Come on, let's get out and tuck in the bed. The covers have come all loose."

I climbed out and knelt, giving a tug to the blanket and sheet from my side. Dinah couldn't bear loose covers. She needed them snug, and I was a thrasher. The hardwood floor always hurt my knees, and there were nights when we tucked ourselves in two and three times. Sometimes I minded, but mostly I didn't. Sometimes Dinah minded, but mostly she didn't either.

Our bed was supposed to be the twins'. But we balked at passing it on to them, and finally Mama agreed they might keep each other awake all night in a double bed, so Dinah and I got to keep it. The twins, Tiny and Bits, were asleep in separate beds across the hall.

The twins were nearly four. Their real names were Christina and Elizabeth, but mostly we called them the twins, as though they weren't two different people at all but were just parts of one whole thing . . . which in a way was true.

"I didn't mean we bought the twins," I said, sliding carefully back under the covers. "It's 'all those mouths to feed.' Maybe that's the trouble. Mama always says the grocery money—"

"I don't think it's a problem about feeding us, Addie, no matter what Mama says."

"Then what?" I asked, winding my feet back through Dinah's.

"I don't know," she said. "Maybe it's everything. Maybe it's nothing."

"The boat!" I said. Daddy had bought us a boat, a big one, forty feet long, with room to sleep eight and everything including radar and venetian blinds. It was glorious, and I loved it. We all loved it. All except Mama, who called it "that floating insanity" and then usually managed to slam something down hard.

In a voice I imagined sounded exactly like Mama's, I said, "That boat's going to land us in bankrupcy court!"

"Addie." Dinah sighed. "Addie, you have to stop. You can't figure out what they're fighting about, because it might not even be about money. They were fighting long before we got the boat. They were fighting before they got *you*. I know, 'cause I was there."

"Then what—"

"Then nothing," Dinah said. "Just nothing. Plug your ears. Do something else. Hum. Just don't listen, and don't try to figure anything out. It's a waste of time. Really, Addie. It's just a big waste of time." She rolled over, away from me, yanking her feet free.

For as long as I could stand it, I lay absolutely still, giving Dinah a chance to fall asleep. I was sorry I'd annoyed her. I listened alternately to her breathing and to my parents' fighting downstairs. Shout, silence, shout, silence. It was lasting forever. Twice I turned, a cautious sliding turn, and later I bunched my pillow around my ears so the only sound I could hear was my own heartbeat—*ba-woosh, ba-woosh, ba-woosh.*

Finally I lifted my head slowly and whispered into the black. "Dinah?"

Silence and then a sigh. "What?" she whispered back.

"Are you asleep?"

"No. Are you?"

"No, I can't. Dinah, is he going to leave?"

"I don't know. Anyhow, if he does leave, he'll come back. He always does. So go to sleep, okay?"

"I tried," I said.

"Try harder."

"I did that, too."

Another sigh, then she rolled toward me. "Turn on your stomach," she said. "I'll scratch your back."

"Really?" I was over in a flash.

"But only if you promise to keep your eyes closed. And no more questions about *them.*"

"Promise," I said.

Dinah began an aimless kind of scratching all around my back, then brushed quickly and lightly all over, like you'd smooth sand on a beach. Then, starting in the center, she scratched a spiral. It felt delicious.

"Do you want a story?" she asked.

"Oh, yes. A trip!" The trip stories were the best.

"To Disneyland?" she asked.

"No, someplace we've really been. I can imagine it better if we've really been there."

"Okay," she said, "here goes. It's summer, and Daddy and you and me are going on a trip."

"On the boat!" I guessed. Mama hardly ever wanted to go on the boat.

"No, not this time, Addie. Anyhow, I'm telling

the story, and you can't butt in. Just let me tell it. I'll make it good—you'll see."

She began again. "It's summer, and Daddy and you and me are going on a trip. It's going to be a long trip, and Mama doesn't want to go, because the twins get too bored in the car. And anyhow, she doesn't like Nevada."

"The ranch!" I knew it! This was just as good as the boat, only different.

"Shh," Dinah said. "Now, this is you." She began sketching on my back. "This is your curly hair, these are freckles, since it's summer, and here is your suitcase." All along she sketched as she talked, drawing anything that suited her fancy—the road, a tree, the nozzle on a gas pump.

"We're both strapped in the front seat, since neither one of us wants to sit in back. And here we go across the San Mateo Bridge—*zoom*—up and down and over the water and off. No toll. And here we go on the interstate, which is very boring so I'm going to speed some here just to get it over with. *Zoom, zoom.* And we get all the way to Auburn, and now it's very hot, so Daddy stops to buy us all soft drinks. This is your Coke. This is fizz. And he says, 'Don't tell your mother about the soft drinks, or she'll skin me. It's supposed to be lemonade!' So we swear and cross our hearts and laugh every time we have one.

"When we get all the way to Truckee, we stop for lunch. Daddy says, 'Boy, the air sure is thin at six thousand feet,' and we twirl in circles with our arms out trying to feel how thin it is. Twirling. But it feels just the same to us. When we get to Reno, Daddy buys us each a roll of quarters to put in the slot machines, and I quit with a five-dollar profit, and you lose all of yours."

I groaned while she drew the slot machine, because this was a true story and some parts I wished she'd skip.

"And then we're back on the interstate again because Daddy says he wants to get there before dark—only he goofs and calls it 'home' and he's in this really great mood. The whole way we've been listening to country stations, and we're not supposed to tell Mama about that either, although I can't think what's wrong with listening to Merle Haggard sing.

"Then finally we turn off the interstate onto a plain paved road, and off that to another, and then to a dirt road, and our teeth shake nearly out of our heads. We leave a big dust cloud behind the car, and once we hit a tumbleweed and it explodes! It actually explodes to bits! And Daddy points to the horizon and says, 'There. Those are ours.' We can't make out what he's pointing at for the longest time until finally we can see they're sheep. Maybe a thousand. All bunched together because sheep like it that way even when there's lots of space.

"And then we're at the ranch. Grandma gives us hugs, but she and Grandpa don't act really excited to see us. Instead they just take up talking to Daddy as though he'd last been there this morning instead of three years ago, and he seems to like this, although I would have preferred a fuss. We go to sleep in the attic room under the open window with the whole Milky Way blazing right up there in the desert sky.

"The next morning Daddy takes us out to ride

Damnhorse. But I refuse to ride when Daddy says he's called Damnhorse because he won't mind anybody. You don't care, though. You get right on without even a saddle, just a bridle and reins, and you ride around all morning and Damnhorse does everything you want him to! Nobody can believe it. Daddy is so excited and proud that in the afternoon he takes you in Grandpa's pickup the back way into Winnemucca and gets you a real cowboy hat. You choose black. Now why would anyone choose black?

"I shouldn't tell you this, but I spent the whole rest of that trip trying to get up the nerve to ride Damnhorse. Only I just couldn't do it. He was so big—and mean, too, I think, the way he stood on your foot for so long that afternoon and wouldn't budge. So I got Grandma to teach me to make buttermilk pancakes the way Daddy likes them, and the morning that you and Daddy went with Grandpa to look for the lost lambs . . ."

I never did hear the rest of Dinah's story that night, because she had finally soothed me to sleep. I'd forgotten all about the argument downstairs, which must have ended sometime while Dinah was talking and zooming down the highway and sketching tumbleweeds. And there never was a slamming door either, because it turned out Daddy didn't leave that night after all. Instead, he left the next morning. And this time he left for good.

Two

At first it seemed like nothing had changed. Mama did what she always did when Daddy stormed out: she cleaned. She'd clean furiously for a day, a few days, until he came back.

This time she started cleaning and didn't stop. She did the windows and under all the furniture and took everything out of the kitchen cupboards and washed the shelves. She did laundry every day. The hamper was always empty; every sock was matched and in a drawer. She scrubbed the kitchen floor with a hard brush and used lemon-smelling stuff on the furniture. Even the twins were shiny. When Tiny spilled juice on her shirt, Mama hustled her into the bedroom for a change of clothes. She was always chasing one or the other of them with a damp rag.

At first all the cleaning made me feel good. Everything was in order, and Daddy would be coming back soon. But four days passed and then six and then two weeks, and still Mama cleaned. And she had just begun.

She didn't talk much when she cleaned. She

never did. Mostly she gave orders. "Don't drop your backpack on the couch. Take it to your room where it belongs." "Put that tissue in the trash." She didn't say there was a rule not to talk about other things, but you knew. And most of all, we shouldn't mention Daddy.

You wouldn't believe, really, the places there are to clean that you never think of. Mama took pictures off the walls and vacuumed the backs. She used a toothbrush to scrub the spaces between the bathroom tiles. The kitchen stove was apart in pieces for two days. This wasn't like any housecleaning I had ever seen before. This was beyond all clean.

It was spring, and all the while Dinah and I went back and forth to school just like we always did, as though nothing had changed. And part of me thought nothing *had* changed. After all, I knew how the cleaning would end—it would end with Daddy coming in the door. Only this time it was taking longer.

For some reason it kept on raining even though the rainy season should have been over, and I wore a raincoat to school most days. My shoes never got all the way dry.

I made sure I was ready to leave for school in the mornings when Dinah did so I wouldn't have to walk the nine blocks alone. They were a long nine blocks, down Maybeck Road, then around and up Arroyo where it curled past the canyon, then across Wildwood to school.

The no-talking rule seemed to follow us out of the house. We walked in silence. But we were together. I listened to the sound of our sneakers on the wet pavement and played a little game with myself, trying to match my footsteps exactly to Dinah's so that it would sound like one person walking along the road. One big person, instead of two small ones. Sometimes it worked.

When we got to school, Dinah would hesitate for a moment and turn and give me a smile. It was a little smile, tight. Like someone had stitched it. But I waited for that smile and then I went to class.

Then in the afternoon, even though the fifth grade ended half an hour later than second grade, I waited until Dinah got out so we could walk home together. I just wanted to be near her. All the time. I stuck to her like glue.

One day on the way home, the silent way home, I couldn't stand it any longer.

"When do you think he's coming back?" I asked.

Dinah jumped as though someone had just set off a firecracker. "Who?" she said. As if she didn't know.

"Daddy." *Of course, Daddy.*

"He's not coming back."

"Mama thinks he is," I said.

"What makes you say that?"

"Because of how she's acting," I said. "All the cleaning. It's what she always does until he comes home."

Dinah shook her head. "Mama's just . . ." She stopped. Stopped talking and stopped walking. She just stared, at nothing.

"What? Mama's just what?"

"I don't know," Dinah said. "I don't know what Mama's doing. And I don't know what she thinks.

But if she thinks he's coming back, I think she's wrong."

"Why?" I asked.

"Oh, for heaven's sake, Adelaide!" She walked on. Marched, more like.

I scrambled after her. "But Dinah . . ."

"Use your head! You were there, Addie. You saw everything. You know. He's not coming back."

I had been there. And I did see everything. I saw, and Dinah saw, and the twins saw.

And this time it *was* different. He hadn't stormed out in the night. He'd waited until morning and had packed a suitcase. Two suitcases. And a small carton with papers from his study.

I didn't see him pack, because I guess it was early in the morning, before I was up. So what I saw was when I was dressed and about to start downstairs. He was at the bottom of the staircase, with a suitcase in one hand and the box in the other arm and the front door was open, blowing a draft right up to where I stood.

Mama's face was angry. Furious. It was a face made out of concrete, nothing soft anywhere.

"You can't do this to me again," she said. I don't know how she said that without opening her mouth, but she did.

Daddy shook his head and looked away from her, out the door. "I won't," he said. He jammed the box under his arm and picked up the other suitcase and then stood upright. Very upright. He looked Mama in the eye and said in a voice that was as stiff and straight as he stood, "I won't be doing this again, Barbara. This is the last time. This time I'm not coming back."

So I was there, yes. And I saw. And it's not so much that I remember what happened as that I remember every thread in my father's jacket, and the way my mama's two gray hairs curled against the brown, and how Bits was holding Tiny by the strap of her coveralls and Dinah's hand stopped midair just as she reached for the banister.

Everything. I remember it all. Just as if someone had clicked a big three-dimensional camera, and it's all there in my mind where I can look at it any time I want just in case I forget some small detail. Which I never will.

So how come I didn't know?

Dinah's march was quick, and I felt like she was trying to get away from me. But I stuck with her, and in a minute when it seemed like she might have cooled down I said, "But what does Mama think? That's what I want to know." And to myself I added, *Because if Mama thinks he's coming back, then maybe . . .*

"I don't know!" Dinah said. "I don't know what Mama thinks, and if you want to know then maybe you'd better ask her yourself! But I'm warning you, Addie—before you do, you'd better be sure just how bad you need to know."

I stayed right with her the rest of the way, until we were nearly home and I could see the poplar tree in our front yard, up the road just past the bend. And I thought about how much I wanted to know about Daddy. And how much I didn't want to ask Mama myself. So before we could get any closer to home, I took a deep breath.

"Could you be the one to ask?" I said.

More firecrackers. A bunch this time. *"No!"* she yelled. "Absolutely not! Addie, I don't want to know. I don't need to know. There is nothing about Daddy I need to know bad enough to go asking Mama questions. So leave me out of this!"

She took off running and got into the house with the door shut behind her before I was even near.

I took my time, then. My mind wasn't made up. That's what I told myself as I stalled out front. Maybe I'd ask Mama my question, maybe not. If I wanted to, if I *felt* like it, then maybe. Otherwise . . .

I closed the front door behind me and stood on the heel of one shoe to get it off.

"Leave your shoes in the front hall," Mama called. "I don't want mud in here."

I did. I knew. Then I took the rest of my stuff to the family room and set my backpack on my chair at the dining table.

The twins were playing with toys on the floor—one of their new games I didn't understand where they both talked at once, soft and low.

"Hi, you two," I said, and rumpled the hair of each twin.

They turned and looked up at me, an empty look, their eyes big and sunk in their faces. In a moment Bits smiled, though Tiny didn't. And neither moved. Lately, it seemed, they barely moved at all.

I went to find Mama.

She was drawn on one knee by the paneling next to the fireplace, rubbing the wood with some strong-smelling stuff from a plastic bottle. She didn't turn around when I came in, and I couldn't tell if she even knew I was there, so I just watched her.

Finally, "Mama?"

"Unnh?" She kept on rubbing.

"Can I ask you something?"

"Unnh."

"It's about Daddy."

Her hand stopped at about two o'clock in the circle she was rubbing. Stayed right there, but stopped.

"What I want to know . . . I just was wondering . . . is he coming back?"

The hand with the cloth was stuck right to the wall, but something changed in Mama's breathing. I could see it through her sweatshirt. She heaved. One deep breath, then a couple more. Then she turned so fast my heart jumped. Her eyes were hot.

"Who . . ." she said between breaths, "just precisely who wants him, anyway? Who wants that no good, useless . . . that . . . *Just who wants him, anyway?"*

She flung the rag on the hearth, got to her feet, and ran from the room. She ran all the way up the stairs, and then I heard her bedroom door slam.

I stood where I was for a long time—numb, I guess—until finally I realized somebody should screw the lid on the plastic bottle of smelly stuff and put it away where the twins couldn't get it. So I did that.

Then I sat on the couch in the living room for a while and did nothing. Just sat. And when I was done with that, I went into the family room and did the same thing, only at the table. I sat, and lay my head on my arms, and watched the twins play their game.

Maybe, if I'd been paying attention, I could have figured out what the game was about, but I wasn't. I watched, just letting them be there. Then, when they turned on *Sesame Street,* I watched that with them.

Some long while later Dinah showed up and said that Mama wasn't coming down and we would have to fix the dinner. I didn't know a thing about fixing dinner, and I wasn't sure Dinah did either, but I opened and closed a lot of cupboards with Dinah until finally she muttered into the refrigerator, "I don't know how to cook any of this stuff. It's going to have to be tuna."

Tiny and Bits came and stood right behind Dinah at the counter, so close to each other that they touched from the shoulders down. Tiny shook her head. "I just don't," she said. "No, I don't."

"What?" Dinah asked. "You don't what?"

"It's tuna," Bits said. "We don't eat tuna. We don't like it."

"But I've already opened this," Dinah said. Then she sighed. "Never mind. You'll like it this time, promise. I'll fix it so you'll like it."

She put in mayonnaise and relish. And chocolate chips. Then she served it all on a plate with soda crackers and applesauce and the twins ate every bite. So did Dinah. So did I. I smacked my lips and said "Mmm," although you'd have to eat chocolate chips in tuna to know just how bad it really is.

When it was getting dark and Mama still hadn't come down, Dinah decided we should put the twins to bed. This part I knew about, because I had helped before. It went faster with two people. Toilet, teeth, then zip them into their sleepers. You had to get it done before they were too tired; otherwise, it was like trying to fit sleepers on a pair of wet noodles.

That's when Mama came in, just at the zipping part. "I can finish up here," she said. "But I'd appreciate it if you two girls would clear up in the kitchen. I'm tired."

She looked tired, too. Her face was puffy, and she had dark circles under her eyes. She didn't really seem to see any of us.

I followed Dinah downstairs, and it was while I was shaking cracker crumbs from the twins' place mats into the sink that Dinah said, "What did you do to her, anyway?"

That was exactly how she asked the question, like I had done something to Mama. And I couldn't answer at first, because I suddenly knew that I had done something. Something bad.

"I don't know," I mumbled.

"Well, what did you *say?*"

"Nothing, really," I said. "Well, I mean I only asked about Daddy. Whether he was coming back."

"I warned you," Dinah said. "You see? You should never have asked."

I didn't know what to say to that, so I didn't say anything. Dinah ran the water hard over the dishes in the sink and poured in a lot of soap. The suds rose up over the edge. I got a dish towel and dried as Dinah washed.

There were still suds left when she pulled the plug, and for some reason we both stood there watching them pop and fizzle until they were mostly gone.

Then Dinah asked, softly so I nearly didn't hear her, "So what did she say?"

"About Daddy, you mean?"

"Uh-huh."

"Not much," I said. "That is, she didn't really answer my question. She just said, 'Who wants him?' and went upstairs."

Dinah shook her head. "That's the answer, then," she said. "That's the whole, entire answer." As if that cleared everything up.

Sleep came hard that night. I didn't want to thrash, because it seemed like I'd already made trouble enough for everybody, but holding still took a powerful will.

I kept seeing Mama, sometimes in frozen frames and sometimes in moving video, her hand stuck against the wall, and her shoulders heaving. And I'd hear her. *Who wants him?*

She hadn't answered my question, no matter what Dinah thought. And there was another question I wanted an answer to. Where was he? I hadn't seen him for weeks. Or spoken to him. And so far as I knew, neither had anyone else. Although it was possible that Mama had, and simply wouldn't tell us. I had the idea that more of Daddy's clothes and some of his tools had slipped away while Dinah and I were at school, but I wasn't sure—there were still things sitting around that I thought of as belonging to him. Could he really have come and gone and nobody mentioned it, not even the twins, who were home with Mama all the time?

Where was he? Where was he right this very minute, while I lay in bed wondering? I tried to place him, get a picture in my mind of where he might be. But all I could get was a landscape of cracked earth and sagebrush and a tumbleweed bouncing ahead of the wind. No Daddy.

Who wants him? A question for an answer. But it was a question that I happened to have an answer to. Because I, for one, did.

Three

By late June, the place in me that was pretty sure Daddy wasn't coming back was bigger than the place in me that thought he might. So much had changed, for one thing.

Mama had changed from a person of varied dispositions to a person of all one mood. She was angry. And when she wasn't angry, she seemed right on the verge of it. You didn't want to annoy her if you could help it.

It wasn't a matter of keeping mud out of the house anymore, because the rains had long since stopped. And so had the cleaning frenzy. She never went back to it after the night of the chocolate-chip tuna, and the paneling on one side of the fireplace was evermore shinier than on the other.

It was easier to live in a house that didn't have to be kept spotless. And I think I would have felt good about the change if Mama had become more of her old self, more relaxed. But it was more like she just wasn't interested, and there was nothing relaxing about that. I found out that *You can make a mess because it's okay* was worlds away from *You can make a mess because nobody cares.*

What Mama cared about seemed to exist solely at the other end of a telephone, and she wanted to be alone to use it. She talked mostly to friends, which I knew because sometimes I would answer or Dinah would answer and call out. But once or twice when she was in her room, I thought she might be talking to Daddy. I thought so because I would hear her get really mad and yell some, and I couldn't think of anyone else she yelled at like that.

She spent the most time talking to Marta Siewald, which was strange in a way because she'd never liked Marta all that much before. Marta was a single mother, and I wondered if that was why Mama was so interested in her now.

For a while I worried that Mama would start inviting her over to dinner. Because if Marta came to dinner, so would her daughter, Lizzy. Lizzy was in my second-grade class, and there was something goofy about her, like she didn't have good sense. I didn't think I was up to Lizzy. Not lately. But I needn't have worried, because Mama didn't seem to be up to guests herself. She barely cooked for us.

Dinnertime would come, and sometimes if Mama had been holed up in her room on the phone for a long time, Dinah would send me in to ask if we should fix something for ourselves. Usually Mama would say, "No, I'll come," and then she would. In time. But sometimes I'd stick my head in the door and Mama would cover the receiver with one hand and just say, "Out!" Or she'd shoo me with a wave of her hand. I hated that. It made me feel like a bug.

One afternoon while Mama was in the laundry room—she still *did* the laundry; she just didn't fold it anymore; she dumped it on the family room couch and left it—Dinah answered the downstairs phone. She raced into the laundry room and hollered, "Mama, quick, it's Mr. Ramos."

Mama made a dash all the way up the stairs and then called from her room, "I've got it, Dinah. You can hang up now."

"Who's Mr. Ramos?" I asked.

Dinah looked at me and then slid her eyes away. "Nobody," she said.

That struck me as an outright lie, and I was startled. I don't think Dinah had ever lied to me before.

"He must be somebody," I said. "If he's nobody, how come you said 'quick,' and how come Mama ran all the way to her room?"

"If I tell you, you have to promise not to tell anyone," she said.

"Okay," I said, "promise."

"He's the lawyer."

A lawyer. *The* lawyer. Lawyers were for going to jail. What was going on? "Why would a lawyer call Mama?"

"About the divorce," Dinah said. "He's the lawyer for the divorce." She said it in that way Dinah had sometimes of making all of her words sound like they'd been run over by a steamroller. A squashed-flat kind of talking.

Of course I knew about divorce. I had even let the word float around in my mind when I thought about Mama and Daddy. But this time I *felt* it. Right in the stomach, like a giant knot.

"A divorce? Are they getting a divorce? And

why is it a secret?" The questions just rolled out, and more I didn't ask. Like whose idea this was. And what about *me?*

"I don't know," Dinah said, still all squashed flat. "All I know is you can't tell Daddy about Mr. Ramos. That's what Mama said."

Tell Daddy? "Tell Daddy? How could I tell Daddy? I don't even know where he is!" I was so mad so fast, and tears were streaming down my cheeks, and I likely would have hit someone if I just knew who had made me feel this way. The knot had turned into a sharp pain that went right through the middle of me and out the back.

And just that fast Dinah was mad, too. She yelled, "Leave me alone!" and bolted out the back door, letting the screen slam behind her.

I ran up to our room and closed the door behind me, then went into our closet and shut that door, too, and sat on lumps of shoes in the dark and just cried. I cried until I was done. It took awhile.

That night while I was falling asleep—and I wasn't thrashing for a change, maybe because I was so worn out—Dinah started sniffling. It was so quiet at first that I almost missed it, but she didn't stop. And she was making little jerking movements, just every now and then. Dinah was crying.

I didn't have to ask her why. I knew why. I just let her be at first, but when she kept on sniffling I reached out and lightly stroked her hair. I did that until she fell asleep. And then I kept doing it until I fell asleep.

But Dinah didn't just cry herself to sleep that night. She did it the next night, and the night after that. She did it every night for so long that more than once I thought she'd cry herself to sleep for the rest of her life. Come daylight she was okay, and she never mentioned the nighttime weeping, so I didn't either. Our family was getting expert at not mentioning things.

Mostly Mama stayed on the phone or in her room. She'd venture out a couple of times a day to do the minimum, dishes or cooking and a little straightening. And she went to the store, although she no longer bothered to change out of her sweatclothes first.

Often she took Dinah and left me to watch the twins. There was nothing to this job. The twins were quieter than ever. They looked more at each other than anything around them, and they seemed to be getting the knack of taking care of themselves, of each other.

Gloom and upset had seeped like some kind of thick fog into every corner of our house. And it stayed there for an entire month, until Owen came to visit.

It was a Saturday morning when the phone rang, and Mama answered it in the kitchen. I was standing nearby with a slice of cheese in my hand, and I heard her, sounding lifeless at first, say, "Oh, hi, Owen. . . . I'm fine. . . . No, really, I'm okay. The same, you know. . . ."

And then, sounding more bright, "Yes . . . oh, yes, I'd like that. . . . No, I'd really like it, Owen. I could use the company." And then, almost alarmed, "Well, no, I hadn't made any plans. . . . No, of course I didn't forget—I just hadn't made plans yet. There's still time. . . . Well, of course, that would be perfect. They'd love it. We'd all love it." And she turned to me and beamed a warm smile, and I didn't know why that startled me until I realized how long it had been since I'd seen one.

"The twins' birthday," she said to me when she hung up. "It's day after tomorrow—did you forget?" And then she didn't wait for an answer. "Go find Dinah. And the twins. Your uncle Owen is coming down from Turlock, and we have a lot to do. Oh, my . . . this house . . . it's a wreck. How will we ever . . .?" She ran a hand through her hair, looked around, then made a grab for a pile of newspapers on the family-room couch.

Wherever Mama had been for the last four months, she suddenly came back and put us all to work. And I don't think anyone minded. This wasn't like her silent, furious cleaning of weeks before. She was one of us, in charge and looking forward.

Even the twins churned from room to room on their almost-four-year-old legs, making deliveries—a sweater to a bedroom, the stapler to the study. Mama swept; Dinah carried out sacks of trash. I spent a full hour on a pot that had sat for a week in the sink.

Mama was rubbing scouring powder around on the kitchen counter when something out the window caught her eye and she froze.

"The yard," she said. "Would you look at that, Addie?"

I had to boost myself on the edge of the counter to see, and then it was a minute before I knew what she was talking about, even though it was perfectly obvious. "It's all weeds," I said.

"*Dry* weeds," she said. "We can't have a barbecue out there—it'll go up in flames." Then, almost to herself, she said, "I wondered when that happened?"

I knew when it had happened. Daddy was the one who always mowed the lawn and ran the sprinkler in the dry season. The yard had gone to weeds since he'd left. It happened while we were waiting for him to come back and take care of it.

First thing Sunday morning, Mama went next door and got Mr. Lesure to show her how to start the lawn mower. I sat with Dinah and the twins on the front steps and watched.

The mower coughed and sputtered and kept dying at first, and Mr. Lesure said, "I've thought, more than once, of offering to come do this lawn for you, Barbara."

"Oh, no," Mama said. "I appreciate it, but it isn't necessary, really. I've been *meaning* to do it. I've just had a lot on my mind. You know. I mean, Lucas is gone—I don't know if you heard about that." She looked around uneasily, then down at her feet.

"I noticed he wasn't around. I'm sorry, Barbara." Mr. Lesure gave another tug on the rope and the mower sputtered again. "It's just that your yard . . . well, it doesn't look well in the neighborhood, if you take my meaning. Property values. You understand."

Mama glanced over at us with a little frown. You could tell she didn't like hearing she was running down the neighborhood.

The mower caught and held, and Mama bent over and watched while Mr. Lesure talked about the choke, and then she thanked him and waved him away and she was off.

Dinah and I raked and stuffed weeds into plastic

sacks, and it took the better part of the morning what with the mower dying every few feet in the high, dry grass. But finally it was done. It didn't look just like every other yard on our street even then. Ours was all brown and patchy. But Mama said it would come back, and she left me and Dinah to water while she cleaned up and took the twins to shop.

We hosed off the picnic table, hauled the barbeque grill from the garage, and hosed that off, too, and when Mama came back she had bags and bags of groceries and matching yellow dresses for Tiny and Bits and about a hundred balloons, which I blew up one by one that evening until my cheeks gave out.

Nothing about getting ready for Owen's visit was as hard as waiting for him the next morning. Dinah and I hung all the balloons from strings along the backyard fence, and then we went out to the front yard to wait. I kept craning my neck to see down the road, hoping that the next car would be a green pickup truck with a camper top, and that I'd see it first. And then, when he finally did arrive, it was at the very minute I was in getting a drink, and Dinah had to call for me. So I was last to get there and jump on him.

Picture a tree whose fruit is people, and that's what Owen looked like that morning with all of us hanging on him, including Mama. He was Mama's older brother, and his hair was exactly the same shade of brown except that his was silver at the temples. In all of my memories of him he always dressed the same, in scuffed Redwing boots, blue jeans, and a stained and battered tan Stetson. Only his shirts seemed to come and go.

When we finally let him loose, he went around to the back of the truck and *ta-da'*d out a fanfare and told us all to get ready for the world's best birthday present for the world's best four-year-old twin girls. "Unless your mama makes me take it back," he said with a wink. Then he pulled out a wire cage that was two feet in every dimension and occupied by a mynah bird.

Nobody who saw the twins' faces could ever have made him take that bird back. At the same instant, they each clapped their hands to their cheeks and said, "Ooh . . ." and if they didn't say thank you—which I don't think they did because they were so busy saying, "Hello, pretty bird"—I believe Owen felt thanked.

He carried the cage into the backyard, and it stayed there the rest of the day with us while Owen grilled hamburgers and told stories, some funny and some scary, about his job as a crop duster, and Mama poured lemonade and sipped iced tea and listened to him and laughed—actually laughed out loud, with the sun on her hair and turning her nose pink, and a smear of grease to one side of her chin.

Tiny and Bits mostly hovered over that bird, and Dinah and I did our share, I admit. We cut up slices of apple and banana, which the twins shoved through the bars of the cage. Then they went into one of their huddles where they both talked at once, and when they came out they'd given the mynah a name.

"He's called Lord Rodhopper," Bits announced.

"Lord Rodhopper," Tiny echoed.

And when Dinah asked why Lord Rodhopper, they looked around like we must not know *any-*

thing, until finally Bits said, "Because that's what he *is.*"

Later I heard Mama say to Owen, "I can't imagine what made you think of such a gift, but it must have been inspired."

And he said, "Well, the fact is I was offered him in part payment for a job. I wasn't going to take him at first, but then I thought of the twins, and I thought they might need him. And Lord Rodhopper might need them as well. He's supposed to talk, but the only thing I've ever heard him say is, 'Let me outta here.' " And then Owen slapped his thigh and reared back and laughed so hard his hat fell off, and he said, "I swear to God, it's absolutely true."

Sometime between the hamburgers and the cake, Mama disappeared into the garage and came back pulling a bright red wagon. It was big, the kind with wooden rails on the sides that you can take off, and Tiny and Bits abandoned Lord Rodhopper and climbed right in without even waiting for someone to say it was for them.

"It's from your father," Mama said. The way she said it, it sounded like the wagon was little more than a bar of soap, and Daddy was nobody special.

I was stunned. How had the wagon gotten there? It wasn't in the garage the day before when Dinah and I had hauled out the grill. Or at least I didn't think so. So had Daddy delivered it in the night? Was my father some kind of phantom?

If it had been okay to ask Mama questions, I guess I would have asked. But I knew better. I turned to Dinah to ask her a question with my eyes, but she had an expression that was something like shocked, and maybe wounded, too. I knew she didn't know any more than I did.

I picked up the handle to the wagon and took the twins for a ride. A long ride, in big circles around the yard. And when I got tired of that, Dinah took over. And then when she got tired, the twins took the sides off the wagon, loaded up Lord Rodhopper's cage, and paraded him around the yard. Daddy wasn't mentioned again.

We all sang "Happy Birthday" when Mama brought out the cake, including Tiny and Bits who sang to each other. Mama let us have seconds, and Owen even had thirds, and I guess we would have stayed out there in the patchy brown yard with the balloons on the fence and the evening sun maybe until dark if Tiny hadn't slowly tipped forward and fallen asleep with her cheek in the cake.

We made a procession to put the twins to bed, with Owen carrying Lord Rodhopper, Mama carrying Tiny, Dinah leading Bits, and me bringing up the rear with balloons in each hand.

Owen spent the night on the couch in the family room, and in the morning Mama made waffles. When we were done eating, Mama herded us all off to wash sticky syrup from our hands and to leave her and Owen alone to visit.

I washed up in the downstairs bathroom and was just coming out when I heard Owen say, "Lucas," and stopped dead in my tracks. I wanted to hear anything that was said about Daddy, and I stood there in the small hallway outside the bathroom listening with all my might.

"Well, you're going to have to be realistic," Owen said.

"I *am* being realistic," Mama said. "I've thought

it over and I've talked to a lot of people, and this is what I want to do."

"I understand that, but wanting isn't doing, Barbara. 'If wishes were horses . . .' I don't see how you can hope to keep this huge house and four children unless you have a job. And even then, I don't see it. What's your mortgage payment, anyhow?"

I didn't know then what a mortgage was, so the number Mama rattled off didn't mean anything to me. But it was big, and it meant something to Owen.

"Impossible," he said.

"It's *not* impossible. Lucas will help. He said he would, and even if he hadn't, the lawyer says he has to. So we'll make it. Maybe there'll be a little belt tightening, but . . ."

"You can tighten your belt all the way to your backbone, Barbara, and you'll still be in trouble. That's just a fact. Do you think Lucas is going to give you every penny he owns? He needs to eat, you know."

"Well, I imagine he'll have to sell that precious boat of his," Mama said.

"Even so!" Owen was talking louder, frustrated, I guess. And I was getting a little lost what with tight belts, and wishes that turned into horses, and mortgages, but I stayed put.

"That boat's financed, isn't it?" Owen asked.

"Well, yes . . . but he'll get *some*thing for it."

"Not enough, Barbara, not enough."

There was just a clattering of dishes for the next few moments, and I thought they were done. I was about to leave when I heard Mama blow her nose, and Owen took up again in a softer tone.

"Look, Barbara, I didn't come all the way down here to upset you. It's just that I'm concerned. And the folks are concerned. If you moved back home, you could get a house large enough for the five of you for about half the money. And we'd be around to help with the kids. If you needed to work . . ."

"Stop!" Mama interrupted him. "Just stop. You don't understand, Owen. I could no more move back to Turlock than I could . . . I just couldn't! You *like* the valley—you like the heat and the flat and the endless tule fogs. I don't. I hate it.

"What I want is here. Everything I've always wanted is here. I like living near the coast, I like these hills, I like this neighborhood and this house. And it's perfect for the kids. The schools are good, and the city is less than an hour away, and they can have every opportunity. Dinah's doing so well in school already—she's so bright, you know—she can have the life I never had. They all can. And I've worked so hard for it. Lucas and I both worked for it."

Owen didn't say anything to that for a minute. And then when he spoke, it came out careful, like he might break something. "But Lucas is gone, Barbara, and you can't afford it anymore."

"I can," Mama said. "I will. I'll find a way."

I stood there and listened for a while longer, but Mama just offered Owen some more coffee, and then he started talking about someone he and Mama had known in high school who was now living right next door to him, and I slipped away.

I had to find Dinah.

She was in the twins' room, fussing with them over Lord Rodhopper, and it took some doing to get her alone. And then when I told her about overhearing Mama and Owen, it came out jumbled up.

"I don't think Mama would ever move to Turlock," Dinah said.

"I know," I said. "But Owen sounds worried, and I think maybe we aren't rich after all."

"We're not," Dinah said. She got up from the edge of our bed and started pulling scarves off the dress-up rack, like the conversation was over.

"But aren't you worried, then?" I asked.

Dinah took one of the scarves and draped it around my neck, and the biggest, floppiest hat and plopped it on my head.

"Aren't you?" I asked.

"Oh, Adelaide," she said, "we never were rich. Not really. We just had Daddy."

Owen stayed for two more days after that, and if I should have been worried, there wasn't a hint of it.

He changed the washers in a couple of faucets and spent an entire afternoon under the hood of Mama's car with a wrench. And then he took us all out for a Chinese dinner and afterward sat grinning while Dinah and I put on a play for him of Beauty and the Beast. I got stuck with the part of Beast, but Owen said that in a play good acting counted more than good looks, and I thought he meant me.

When he said good-bye on Thursday morning, he went around twice giving hugs, and I heard him say to Mama, "Call if you need me. I'm not that far away."

The cheer that Owen left behind stuck with Mama for days. And with the rest of us, too. Dinah had stopped crying nights when Owen arrived and didn't start up again. She staged a series of plays, with even the twins in bit parts, and Mama sorted through her wardrobe for fresh castoffs to add to our costume collection.

Sometimes I thought about Daddy and wondered why he didn't come, or at least call. I thought he might like to see one of these plays. He might miss us maybe. But there was nobody to ask, and wondering, if I let it go on too long, could make the knot in my stomach come back. So I'd wonder for a bit and then I'd make myself quit.

Then one night after supper Mama sat at the dining table with a stack of mail and a pad of paper and a pencil. The twins were already in bed, and Dinah and I were watching the family-room TV.

I wasn't paying that much attention to Mama, truthfully, except that I knew she was writing numbers and adding them up. But then she began tapping her pencil and muttering, and I couldn't help but notice her. It was like she was gathering some kind of storm.

She sorted papers into piles, saying, "Yes. No. Yes. No, no. No!" as she went. Then all at once, through her teeth she said, "Damn you, Lucas Dillon, damn you," and she swept the whole mess into a pile, dumped it in a drawer, and stalked from the room.

As I think back on it now, I know that that was the night she left us again. And this time she took Dinah with her.

Four

Maybe it was that remark Mr. Lesure had made about property values, or maybe it was her conversation with Owen, or maybe she just felt like it, but the next morning Mama became a gardener. It was like a fever took hold of her and wouldn't let go. Day after day she worked in the yard until her clothes were soaked in sweat. And when she was done, she'd left her imprint on every square foot of our property.

I'd slept late that first morning, so that by the time I got to the kitchen only Tiny and Bits were there, dawdling over bowls of cereal. When the twins ate, they most often gave the impression that getting full wasn't as important as tasting—savoring—and that sometimes even savoring wasn't as important as moving the food around to see Raggedy Ann at the bottom of a bowl. Getting full, if it happened, was something of an accident.

Bits held up her cup and said, "More juice, Addie?" She turned the cup upside down to demonstrate its emptiness and looked surprised when a drop slid out and landed on the table.

The only juice I could find was frozen, and since Mama sometimes fussed about the amount of sugar in apple juice, I went looking for her to ask if I should make that or the orange juice. I thought she might have gone shopping, until I remembered to look out back. She was working by the fence, turning up clumps of earth with a shovel. And Dinah was right beside her with the heavy rake, pulverizing big clumps into smaller ones.

I padded down the steps in my bare feet and stood where I thought Mama might notice me, waiting for her to stop so I could ask my question. But she didn't stop. Dinah glanced at me and kept right on banging with her rake.

"Mama?" I asked.

No answer.

"The twins want some juice," I said. "Should I make apple or orange?"

"I don't . . ." But she stomped the shovel back into the earth, and finished the answer with a grunt.

Dinah answered for her. "Just do either one, Addie. It doesn't matter. Apple is okay."

I went in and made apple juice and didn't think much of it. Then I hung around with the twins for most of the morning and was just beginning to get bored when Dinah came in about noon and asked me to help her make sandwiches.

We made peanut-butter-and-jelly for the twins, then three more with lettuce and sliced turkey, and put them all on plates. Dinah put the twins' plates on the table, and I was bringing two more plates when Dinah said, "No, just one. I'm taking Mama's and mine outside."

"Are you coming back later?" I asked. "Do you want to do a play or something?"

"No," Dinah said. "Mama really needs my help out there. We're putting in a garden."

I partway wanted to say, "Can I help?" and partly I felt I had just been uninvited, so I hesitated, trying to sort that out. And then, while I was hesitating, Dinah said, "Mama says after lunch you should wash the dishes so the kitchen won't be a mess at suppertime."

I'd washed dishes before, of course, but always with somebody nearby to help. This time I did them alone, and as I filled the drainer with them, one by one, I found myself feeling resentful toward each dish, and then toward Mama, and then toward Dinah.

Dinah and Mama worked in that garden for all of August. They soaked the lawn with water until it came back green, and trimmed bushes and turned up earth and pulled weeds and put in baby plants. In the evenings, after supper, they pored over seed catalogues and picked out seeds that might plant in the spring, and flowers that would bloom in the fall—this fall, maybe, if they got them in the ground right away—the bulbs that could go in the ground now and would come up each spring, year after year. They made maps of the land around the house and filled in dots with colored pencils and talked about which areas got the most light, and where shade fell earliest in the afternoon.

I came to hate that garden. That garden, and all gardens, really. I'd look at a garden, and where someone else might see a swatch of beauty, I'd see a place where I didn't belong. A place that sucked up people I cared about and left me standing on the outside.

I wandered around the house unsure of what to do with myself. I'd think of something, and then just as quick as I thought about it I'd realize that it was something I wanted to do with Dinah and she wasn't there. I watched TV, and then when I was sick of that I'd go watch the twins. But they were getting quiet and big-eyed again, and as often as not they'd stop a game if I showed up and just sit still, staring.

Sometimes I watched Mama and Dinah out a back window. I could see them kneeling side by side in the dirt, and they'd dig and scrape and then they'd stop and talk to each other, Mama doing most of the talking, and Dinah listening, nodding, intent. It seemed like more talk than you'd need just to stick a few plants in the ground, and I began to wonder what was going on between them.

One morning I convinced myself that it had all been a mistake—that if I'd just shown more interest in helping with the garden, I could have been included. So I pulled on shorts and a T-shirt and went outside.

I came up behind them while they were weeding a flower bed near the garage, and I hadn't meant to creep, but I guess I did, because when I said, "Hi," they both jumped.

"I just was wondering if you'd like some help," I said.

Mama looked around like she was confused, and Dinah only glanced at me and then back at Mama.

"Well, I don't . . . I'm not sure," Mama said. And then, "Well, yes, Addie, actually you could help. If you'd just take that spray attachment there by the back steps and go and hook it up to the hose in the front yard and water all the flower beds, that would be fine. But use a gentle spray so you won't wash the soil away from the roots. Could you do that?"

"Sure!" I said. I could do that easily. And I felt so much better right away, because all I'd needed to do, after all, was just ask.

I spent quite awhile watering in the front, and even felt somewhat friendly toward the plants until I realized that this wasn't exactly what I had in mind. I was still alone, in front, while Mama and Dinah were together around by the garage.

I finished up with the watering, and then went back to Mama and tried again.

"I'm done," I said. "Is there something I could do to help here? With you and Dinah?"

Mama pulled off a gardening glove and poked a strand of hair back into her bandanna and seemed to be considering. And then she said, "Well, no, Addie, there's nothing we need here right now. But I'll let you know, okay?"

"Okay," I said. And I just hung around watching for a while, waiting, I guess, until it seemed like she hadn't meant soon, and I left.

That afternoon I offered to give the twins a ride in the wagon, and after we'd gone all the way around both the front and back yards, I pulled them down the driveway to the road. And then I took the wagon around the block, or what counted as a block since none of the streets in our neighborhood were anything like square. It meant I had to cross Maybeck Road at Arroyo, but I was careful and looked both ways twice.

The twins loved the ride and told Mama about

it, and she said, "That's nice," so I thought it must be okay. After that I took them for a ride nearly every day. They looked forward to those rides, and pretty soon it got so that if I didn't offer one, they'd come asking.

One early morning as Dinah was dressing, I said, "What do you and Mama talk about when you're working in the garden?"

"Things," Dinah said. She tugged at the laces of her shoe.

"Like what?" I asked.

She shoved her foot into her other shoe and without even looking at me said, "Grown-up things, Addie. It's nothing you would understand." Then she tied that shoe and left the room.

I thought about that on and off for most of the day, wondering what sorts of things Dinah might understand that I wouldn't, and wondering if this meant that Dinah had become a grown-up. If so, I imagined that it had happened out in the garden. I just didn't know how.

I guess this was still on my mind when I took the twins in the wagon that afternoon, because I somehow wandered farther than I meant to, until all at once I was no longer absolutely sure of the way back home. I got scared, then, afraid we were truly lost, and I worried what Mama would think of me if we were. I suppose it would have made sense to stop and ask directions, but I never thought of that then. I didn't want to let on I was lost and maybe scare the twins, so I just kept moving, and my fear kept growing, until almost by accident I came to a street whose name I recognized and finally found our way home.

Bits said, "That was the *best* ride!" But my

heart pounded for days, whenever I thought about it.

We did see Daddy again, before the end of summer. Just before Labor Day, in fact. Mama told us the night before that he would be coming to pick us up, but because she said it in exactly the same tone of voice you'd use to tell someone they had an appointment with the dentist, I almost didn't register that she'd said "your father." *My father.* Daddy. The person who had disappeared and who was now going to reappear. The person I had missed.

He showed up in the very early morning with a new car, so I didn't even know who it was until he'd turned off the engine in the driveway. That shouldn't have surprised me, because Daddy's cars were always changing. It was Mama's car that stayed the same. Daddy sold cars for a living, and the company he worked for always gave him a new one to drive. He once said that was because you couldn't sell a car you didn't believe in enough to drive yourself, and he always believed in his cars.

He must have, because he even sold Owen his truck, and I remember Owen saying, "I'm a tough customer, Lucas. I won't buy it if it's not built to last." But he bought the truck and always thanked Daddy afterward for getting him a good deal and a good truck all at the same time.

Mama used to say, "Lucas doesn't so much sell cars as he *enchants* people into them. It's his charm they buy." But that was in happier days, when he still lived with us.

Nobody jumped on Daddy when he got out of

the car, and I'm not sure exactly why. Maybe it was the way he stood there, looking stiff and uncertain, and maybe we caught it from him. Or it might have been Mama in the doorway, stiffer still, and looking at him angrily, like she'd just dared him to do something and he'd gone and done it anyway.

He was wearing tan slacks and a yellow polo shirt and tennis shoes, and he was leaner than I remembered, and suntanned, and after a hesitation he smiled and said, "Hi, you-all."

With that, Mama turned away and slammed the door shut. She always used to get mad when he talked like a hick, and I guess she still did.

We-all said, "Hi."

Then Daddy opened the car doors and waved us in. "Let's get moving here—we have a long day."

I expected Dinah to head for the front seat, and then we'd have had to share, because I wanted to sit there myself. But she surprised me by climbing right in back with the twins and helping Tiny with her seat belt, while Daddy, on the other side, helped Bits. I was still figuring out how mine worked when Daddy got the car started and we were out of the driveway and gone.

It was a quiet car. Nobody said a word until we were all the way down to the highway, when Daddy said, "So . . . how have you girls been?"

I was so relieved he'd said *some*thing that without thinking I said, "Fine, thanks." And then in a second I realized what a lie it was and said, "Well, not so great, really."

"We're *fine,*" Dinah said. "We're absolutely fine." And she said it with such force that there was no mistaking she did not want to be contradicted.

Daddy shot a quick look at Dinah in the rearview mirror and said, "Uh-huh." And then in a minute he said it again, "Uh-huh." And then he said, "Well . . ." and reached over and turned on the radio, and Willie Nelson was right in the middle of singing "On the Road Again," and that seemed just perfect to me. I started to relax then, I think, and to feel like this was really Daddy and not some stranger who just happened to resemble him.

Daddy hadn't said where we were going, and I hadn't thought to ask—hadn't really cared, I suppose—but I knew as soon as we crossed the bay and turned north onto Crow Canyon Road. We were on our way to Rio Vista, on the Sacramento River, to take the boat out.

We pulled into the harbor parking lot at a little past nine o'clock, and Daddy said, "Okay, girls, gather up your things, and remember, no running on the dock." I had only my sweatshirt, but Dinah had a book, as well, and the twins, maybe because we'd left home so early in the morning, had each brought a stuffed animal. We walked ahead of Daddy down the dock and waited, because that was the rule, for him to catch up and help us on board.

But when I turned around, he'd stopped, some ten feet behind us. And he was gazing at the boat with a thoughtful look, almost wistful, and at the black-and-gold script across the stern—*Desert Bloom.* Then he looked at us and blinked, and seemed to snap out of it. He cocked his head and gave a little smile, warm, then caught up and straddled the boat and the dock and swung us one by one on board.

Our life jackets didn't fit anymore—it had been nearly a year since we'd worn them—and I was fiddling with the straps on mine to make it bigger when Daddy said, "We're making a special trip today. We're going to take the *Desert Bloom* all the way down the river, through the Carquinez Straight and out onto San Pablo Bay. And then we're going to keep on going right down the whole length of San Francisco Bay to Palo Alto. How would that be?" He said it like he'd been thinking on it a long time, like it was a speech he'd prepared.

"Great!" I said.

Tiny, who was being cinched into her life jacket by Daddy, turned to Bits and grinned.

And Bits said, "Rabbit's going on a big trip!" meaning her stuffed rabbit, I guess.

Only Dinah didn't look happy. For a minute she didn't say anything, and then she just said, "Why?"

Daddy gave Dinah a quick, hard look again, a look that was partly questioning, and then he looked away and said, "A new berth, Dinah." And you could tell that if that hadn't answered Dinah's question, it would have to do.

It was a made-to-order day, crystal clear and hot early, and the water sparkled green in the sunlight. Daddy, not seeming to be in any big hurry, took us slowly down the Sacramento. I stood by him at the wheel, and he didn't say much but every now and then nodded his head toward shore for me to look. I knew what he meant. The Montezuma Hills rose off to our starboard side, all soft and golden and lazy, like the flanks of some great lions napping in the sun. And at the shoreline, red-winged blackbirds clung to cattails, swaying. They took to the air in flocks as we passed, and screeched and called and circled to land again.

Tiny and Bits stood on the afterdeck and watched our wake as it spread behind the boat, and Dinah stood there with them for a time. Then she came into the cabin and curled onto a bunk with her book, hardly bothering to look up. Daddy kept glancing back through the cabin to check on the twins on the afterdeck, and each time he did he'd look at Dinah, and concern would cloud his face. I guess he was wondering why she was so pulled into herself, because I was wondering that myself.

Just before we got to the Carquinez Bridge, a barge and tug passed us, headed upriver, and Daddy said, "I've often wondered if I'd have been any good at that."

"At what?" I asked.

"Piloting a tug," he said. "They say the pay's pretty good."

"Don't you like selling cars?" I asked.

Daddy laughed. "Ah, Addie. Liking wasn't even a consideration. I sell cars because I'm good at it, sweetie. And the money is good. But if I could, I'd do work that was closer to my heart. Like standing behind the wheel of that tug, or running sheep in Nevada."

That was just like Daddy, like a person who was forever pulled between two places. Like the boat itself, in fact. He told me once he'd named her *Desert Bloom* because the whole time he was growing up in Nevada he'd dreamed of going to sea. "I suppose that's because there's not enough water in Nevada to make spit," he said. "So this boat is really an idea that bloomed in the desert. Now, of course, there are times when I get a strong yearning for that parched, gritty feel of home." He shook his head then and chuckled. "Some folks you just can't satisfy."

Once we were clear of the bridge and out onto the open bay, Daddy turned to Dinah and said, "Would you like to come take a turn at the wheel, Dinah? I need a few minutes below."

Dinah looked up from her book and shook her head. "No," she said, "I'd rather not."

"Should I ask why?" Daddy said.

"I just don't want to," she said. Then added, "Anyhow, it's too dangerous."

Daddy's jaw dropped at that. "Do you really think I'd ask you to do something dangerous?" he asked.

But Dinah just turned and stared out the portside window and didn't answer.

"How about you?" he said to me. "Would you like to be my first mate? Think you can handle it?"

"Of course I can," I said. I'd done it before. And it wasn't anything like dangerous—I don't know when Dinah'd gotten to be so prissy. Daddy pointed out the channel markers and set the boat on course and asked if I still remembered how close another boat could get before I was to holler for him, which I did. Then he took the twins and went below.

All I had to do, really, was steer the boat in a more or less straight line. And that was just a matter of getting a feel for the wheel again. But I loved it just the same. I think the only other thing that had ever made me feel this big, this *able,* was riding Damnhorse.

He was down below a long time, although I never had to call for him, and when he came up he had a big tray with sandwiches and chips and two kinds of soda and juice.

The twins followed behind, then chattered the whole time they ate about a bird they'd seen that looked just like Lord Rodhopper, and Daddy asked them a lot of questions and laughed and said, "That's some name for a bird."

Dinah took her sandwich and ate it on the bunk without putting her book down, and I noticed she passed up her chance to have a soft drink and had juice instead.

I waited until Daddy was done and took the wheel again before I ate. And then I gobbled, because sometimes food wasn't as important as what else I might be doing. Tiny and Bits were sound asleep on one of the bunks by then. They were like that—they could fall asleep just anyplace if they were tired.

The water on the bay was a deep slate blue and choppy in the wind. For a while I stood out on the deck, but I got hit by spray, and anyway, I really liked it at the wheel. Daddy let me handle the wheel as much as I wanted, but he stayed by me when we got past the Richmond Bridge because the sailboat traffic was heavy.

We were just abreast of Angel Island when I thought of something I wanted to know. And without wondering whether I should, I just came out and asked, "Where do you live now, Daddy?"

"You mean no one told you?" he said.

"No."

"Well, you're standing in it," he said. "I thought you knew."

"The boat? You live on the boat?" I'd never thought of that. I looked around to see if it looked any different. I think I felt it *should* look different. Lived-in, maybe. But it looked the same as always.

"I'm staying on it," he said, "yes. But not for much longer." Then he took a deep breath and said, "I'm selling the *Desert Bloom,* Addie. That's why we're taking her to Palo Alto."

"Oh, no!" I said. I don't know why that made me feel so awful, especially when you could say I'd had some warning. But standing on the *Desert Bloom* and hearing Daddy say he was selling it felt a whole lot different from hearing it in the kitchen at home.

"I'm sorry, kiddo. I was going to wait until we got there to tell everyone. I didn't want to spoil this trip."

"Is it because you need money?"

"Partly," Daddy said. "It's partly that, and partly this boat isn't really meant for living on, and winter will be coming. I need to find a different sort of home, Addie."

"Somewhere near us?" I asked.

I guess I asked that because I wished it, but Daddy didn't answer right away. And then he was vague. "I don't know," he said. "There's a lot going on right now. Lots of things are changing. I'm hoping to get a job with a different company—one that makes more expensive cars. And . . . I just don't know."

"Oh," I said.

I suppose I sounded disappointed, because Daddy said, "Look, Addie, I wasn't going to bring this up today, because nothing is really settled yet. But what I want . . . what I'm hoping for . . . is that eventually I can get a place big enough for you girls to come stay with me. Maybe even live with me sometimes. Would you like that?"

"Oh, yes!" I said.

"Good," he said. "That's good. I'm glad. But now, Adelaide, don't go getting your face all set for it just yet, will you? There are things that have to be worked out, and . . . I just don't know. Nothing's settled right this minute—that's all I'm saying. Do you understand?"

"Yes," I said, although I didn't really. I couldn't understand why Daddy sounded so worried, and I felt uncertain and let down.

I didn't know what else to say right then, and I guess neither did Daddy. After a time he put an arm around my shoulder and said, "Look up ahead, Addie. There's the mighty Bay Bridge. Do you want to be the one who takes the *Desert Bloom* under her?"

The mighty Bay Bridge. I liked the sound of that. And if Daddy meant to make me feel better, he'd succeeded. Even Dinah put down her book long enough to come forward and crane her neck back as we passed under it. She didn't say anything about the conversation I'd had with Daddy, though. And I'm perfectly sure she heard every word.

The sun was low in the sky when Daddy carefully backed the *Desert Bloom* into her new berth. You have to be in about six places at once when you dock a boat, so Dinah and the twins and I stayed out of the way until everything was lashed tight and shut down. Then Daddy hustled us off to the harbor restaurant for dinner. No good-bye ceremony for the boat, and maybe that was just as well.

I hadn't thought about how we would get home, with the car still up in Rio Vista, but luckily Daddy had. A pot-bellied man named Ben Thornton came to our table toward the end of dinner and drank coffee and talked to Daddy while we waited for the twins to finish up. Then he handed a set of keys to Daddy and said, "It was nice to meet you, ladies. Your daddy's told me a lot about you."

I liked that—hearing that Daddy talked about us—and I was pretty sure that everything he said was good.

Daddy said, "I won't be long."

"No hurry," Mr. Thornton answered.

My eyes had that boiled feeling you get from spending a day where the sun glares off the water, and on the way home I kept closing them. Then I'd open them again, because I knew that our day with Daddy was almost over and I didn't want to miss a bit of it. But sooner than I'd expected, we were on our way up Maybeck Road and past the curve and into the drive.

The light was on over the porch steps—Mama had left it on, I guess—and Daddy turned off the engine of Mr. Thornton's car and just said, "Well . . ."

I got this urgent feeling, like there was something I wanted to say, but I couldn't come up with it. I just sat there tongue-tied.

Daddy looked around like he wasn't sure what to do next, and then he said, "Well . . ." again, just like he had before, and then all at once we opened car doors and piled out.

I had to get back in for my sweatshirt, which I'd never needed in the first place, and I heard Daddy say, "Where are those stuffed toys? Tiny? Where's your duck, sweetheart?"

"On the boat," Tiny said.

"Oh, no . . ." Daddy groaned.

"Rabbit and Duck are *both* on the boat," Bits said. She sounded very proud of herself.

Daddy ran a hand over his face. "All right, then," he said. "I'll get them back to you somehow. Just don't worry, okay?"

Tiny positively squealed, "Oh, no, don't do that, Daddy. They have to stay on the boat."

"Stay on the boat?" Daddy said. "But they can't . . ."

"They *need* to," Tiny said, and there was a quaver in her voice.

"They *must,*" Bits said. "They *must,* Daddy."

"Now, just slow down here," Daddy said. "Why don't you tell me the reason they must stay on the boat, and maybe I'll understand."

"It's because they like it there, Daddy," Tiny said.

And Bits said, "We asked them, Daddy, and they said they liked it on the boat. They said they didn't *want* to come home. They want to stay on the boat forever."

My father's expression, in the glow from the porch light, was one I had never seen before—a look of sorrow so deep it ran furrows all down his face. He knelt and grabbed one twin in each arm and buried his face between them. "It's all right," I heard him say, his voice stretched and raspy.

"Everything is going to be all right. Rabbit and Duck can stay. They can live on the boat if that's what they really want."

Dinah turned then and ran into the house, without even saying good-bye.

Daddy held on to the twins for a minute; then he kissed each one in the crook of the neck and stood and put a hand on either side of my face and kissed me on the forehead.

"Be good," he said, and I nodded.

Daddy looked up the walk, toward the open doorway, and then he turned slowly back to the car. He sagged a little bit in every joint, like he was coming loose. Seeing the back of him like that sent a stab right through me, and I almost didn't hear him when he said, "Stick together."

"What, Daddy?" I wasn't sure who or what he meant. The car? Himself? Us? The whole world?

"You girls stick together," he said. "You do that, you hear?"

I nodded again, which I realized later was a waste because his back was to me. But neither did he wait for an answer, because I think I looked away for just an instant myself, and then he was gone.

Mama took Tiny and Bits each by a hand when they came in and marched them off to bed. She must have been waiting. And Dinah already had her nightgown on when I got to our room, which struck me as quick work. There was a mirror over her bureau, and she was standing in front of it brushing her hair in short, brisk strokes, as if something depended on doing it in a hurry.

I stepped on the back of one shoe to pull my

foot out, and then sat on the bed and pulled off the other.

"You'll ruin your shoes if you keep taking them off without untying them," Dinah said.

That was more words than she'd spoken to me all day, and I said, "What's *wrong* with you today? You've been so crabby. You were even crabby to Daddy."

"Dope!" she said. "You are such a *dope.* He doesn't care about us, you know!" She slammed the brush down on the dresser and marched out.

The same family that was expert at not saying things was now getting expert at walking out, and I went to bed alone in the dark and hoped I'd fall asleep before Dinah returned. But even though my eyes were tired, my brain was wide awake, and I could hear Mama and Dinah talking from somewhere. Mostly Dinah talking, and Mama exclaiming. Then I heard Mama very plainly say, "Over my dead body!"

I rolled over and stuck my head under the pillow. Whatever they were saying out there, one thing I knew for sure: Daddy did care about us. I could *feel* it. He did care. Which meant that Dinah had told me her second outright lie on this very night.

Five

When I started school that fall, I was relieved to find I'd been assigned to Mrs. Kurtz's class instead of Mrs. Greeley's. I think I partly liked Mrs. Kurtz just because she was so pretty, with masses of wavy hair nearly down to her waist. But also it was whispered around that Mrs. Greeley, who taught the other class, had bad breath and was about to retire. For a while I thought she was going to retire *because* of the breath, which I'd never been close enough to smell but which I imagined was truly horrible if she needed to retire on account of it. But Jody Masters told me that the retiring was on account of her being so mean, or vice versa, and that straightened me out.

Dinah went into the sixth grade, and on the second day she let me know I wasn't to wait for her after school any longer. I asked why, and she said, "Because I want to walk home with Jenny Cassidy, and I don't want you tagging along, that's why."

I was stung. I thought of myself as Dinah's sister and best friend. Next to me, Jenny had always been second. Now, it seemed, I was just someone who tagged along, like a kind of public nuisance. I didn't really count.

I wondered if sixth grade had done this. The sixth graders in our school always did lord it over the younger kids, but if you'd asked me a year ago if Dinah would turn into one of those, I'd have said, "No way." Now I wasn't so sure.

But it was more than school, really. Something was going on with Dinah at home, and with Mama, too, and maybe it had started with the garden, or maybe it started at the dining table on the morning after our boat trip.

I was sitting at my usual place eating toast, which I had just learned how to make for myself, so I was eating a lot of toast. I'd cook two pieces and butter them and slather them with jam while two more pieces were in the toaster. Then I'd butter those. And depending on how hungry I was—because making toast was more important than eating it right then—I might cut one in half and give it to Tiny and Bits.

Mama came to the table with a cup of coffee and half a cantaloupe and set them down on her place mat. Then she took one edge of the place mat and slid it—cup, saucer, the works—down to the other end of the table. She had to reach over the twins to do this, and we all quit eating and stared. Then, when she got to the far end of the table, she sat down. In Daddy's seat.

I think I stopped breathing. It was just as if she'd said out loud, "We're not expecting him back." And I knew that, of course. I did. Still, hearing her say it, *seeing* her say it, was hard. It just didn't stop being hard.

I needed and excuse to leave the table for a minute, and I found it. Milk. But before I pushed back my chair, Mama pointed to her place, to her just-vacated place at the foot of the table, and said to Dinah, "I think you should sit down there from now on."

Dinah went, of course. But what bothered me was something about the *way* she went, the way she sat in Mama's seat. That chair had arms, which the ones on the sides did not, and Dinah took hold of them and lowered herself so slowly, so carefully, and with her head held so erect, that I thought, *The Queen,* and felt a stab of envy.

After breakfast I went into Daddy's study and closed the door and sat in his swivel chair. Just sat, for the longest time, and listened to the silence. The study was a room so small you'd have called it a closet except for the window that looked out on the shady side of the house. Daddy's desk took up most of the space, with only enough room left to swing the door open.

I pulled out the right-hand desk drawer. It was empty. All the drawers were empty, except for the center one, which had four paper clips, a dried-up bottle of correction fluid, and two ballpoint pens, one of which said, WELLINGTON MOTORS—SERVING YOUR NEEDS SINCE 1961. On the wall over the desk was a row of empty hooks, and I struggled to remember what had hung there. A certificate. Two, I think. SALESMAN OF THE YEAR. And a picture of us four girls—I remembered that—me and Dinah with a twin on each of our laps, when Tiny and Bits were still in diapers. Gone. Daddy had them, I supposed.

I put the Wellington Motors pen in my pocket.

And later, when Mama and Dinah were out back, I crept into Mama's room and used her vanity chair to reach the heavy box of family photographs on her closet shelf. I knew what I was looking for, and I found it. A picture of Daddy with me, aged three, in his arms. My hand is on his cheek and my dress is rumpled, and I'm looking somber. And he's looking right back at me, laughing.

And then one more picture, this one of me alone, up on Damnhorse, the black hat hanging low over my ears. I remember the very instant Daddy took that photo. I can look at it and hear the shutter click and see him smiling and his hair blowing up in spikes in the desert wind. Click. Like that.

I shoved the box back up on the shelf and took those two photographs and the pen and put them in my room, on the board underneath my bottom dresser drawer. And what I knew, what I thought at the time was: *I have something I want, and it is hidden and safe.*

And something else I knew: *I am now a thief.*

After the first day of third grade, I never walked to or from school with Dinah again, even if I had to inconvenience myself to avoid it, which I sometimes did.

Mama was distracted all fall. Worried, I guess. Sometimes I felt the worry, and when I did I felt sorry for Mama and the way it hung on her and made her sad. But more often she moved through the house like a hostile stranger, irritable, distant, and preoccupied. It was hard to feel sorry for her then. She was so apart from us . . . so absent . . . I could hardly conjure in my mind the Mama she once had been.

When I came home from school, Mama was on the phone or in the yard, or, more and more often, I'd find her at the dining table with Marta Siewald at her side. They'd be drinking coffee and poring over a growing stack of papers, most of which were headed, WILLIAM M. RAMOS, ATTORNEY-AT-LAW. I tried to read those papers once, and except that I recognized my parents' names, they might as well have been in code.

I kept trying to like Marta, but I couldn't. She had a barking laugh and wore her hair always combed over to one side in a ponytail. The combed strands stood oddly away from her scalp, and they never ever moved, no matter what. She made me think of the edges of things. And even though she was friendly enough, I always felt like an intruder when she was there. She and Mama would clam right up when I came in, and shortly Marta would excuse herself, saying, "I must get home for Lizzy."

I began to want to say it for her. "Hello, Marta. Don't you need to get home for Lizzy?" Mama was nourishing a rude child under her roof, but she didn't yet know it.

The house was cluttered. Sometimes more, sometimes less, but always cluttered. And the twins, in the afternoon, seemed not so much *in* the clutter as they were part of it. They rocked, and the rocking frightened me. They sat on the family-room couch holding hands, unfolded laundry all around them, and rocked and stared straight ahead. Their heads bounced against the soft back of the couch, and their hair spread behind in static-electric halos.

I came in once and found clean laundry strewn

across their laps, and I never knew if they'd gathered it there themselves or whether Mama had absentmindedly dumped it on them. I was afraid to ask.

After school I took them for wagon rides or dragged chairs to the kitchen counter and helped them spread cream cheese on crackers. I even showed them my schoolwork, and explained it just as though they'd understand. I had to show somebody.

Owen saved the day by mail. He wrote to Tiny and Bits with very specific instructions, gleaned, he said, from the previous owner, on how to teach that mynah bird to talk. Which was a relief, because Lord Rodhopper was forever saying, "Let me outta here!" He said it so often, and sounded so desperate, that the twins had let him out three times. And he was *very* hard to catch.

We fed him his favorite food, grapes, and each time Tiny or Bits stuffed a grape through the bars of his cage she'd say, "I love you so-o-o-o much!" Owen swore it would work, though it took so long I had my doubts. Tiny and Bits believed that sincerity counted, and they threw their whole hearts and souls into that one sentence. *I love you so-o-o-o much!*

But Lord Rodhopper was slow, and Tiny and Bits took to feeding grapes to each other as well. The one who received the grape said it this time, "I love you so-o-o-o much," rewarding the giver. And sometimes the grape spilled back out with the words, sending them both into fits of giggles. I spent a lot of time in the twins' room that fall, sometimes catching the giggles and repeating those words myself. *I love you so-o-o-o much.*

Mama started to complain about the price of grapes. She was complaining about the price of a lot of things. She said we had to cut back on extras and be careful not to waste. And she meant it. She found sixteen different ways to cook rice and beans, and you could get yelled at if you used a paper towel when a sponge would do the job as well.

Dinah, meaning to help Mama, I suppose, made it her mission to find waste and put a stop to it. She turned into a one-person detective bureau . . . and I was her prime suspect. I lost too many pencils at school, and she told me so. I drank milk between meals when water would do, and forgot to turn out the bathroom light. I always, always forgot to turn out the bathroom light.

It wore on me, being dogged by Dinah, until I got mad on the day she brought up my shoes again. I was ruining perfectly good shoes by refusing to untie them before taking them off.

I didn't think they were ruined, but instead of saying that, I said, "You don't know what you're talking about, Dinah."

Dinah snatched up the shoes and marched off to Mama, and in a minute Mama called me into her room.

"These are getting all broken down at the heel," she said.

"I know," I said. "But they're not ruined, and it's quicker to get them on and off if I don't untie them every time."

"But they *will* be ruined. And, Adelaide Dillon, I can't afford to go buying new shoes just because you're too lazy to tie them properly."

"Except you don't!" I said. "You buy me new

shoes when the soles wear out or when my feet get too long. So I don't see what it matters."

Mama furrowed her brow at that. Then she just handed the shoes back, and I was about to leave when Dinah said, "And she's wasting shampoo, too."

And. "I am not!" I said.

"You are," Dinah said. "You always use about three times as much as you need to."

"I don't," I said. "I use *exactly* as much as I need. I use less than you!"

I had no idea how much shampoo I used, or how much Dinah used either, for that matter. I'd never thought about it. But Dinah said, "I have to use more. My hair's longer!"

"See?" I said. I was sure this proved something.

"Mama, she just doesn't want to cooperate," Dinah said. "Every time I tell her not to waste something, all she does is argue."

"That's not true!" I yelled. "I just don't know why you have to bug me every minute. You're not my boss!"

"Dinah's helping because I asked her to," Mama said. "And it's true, Addie, you haven't been cooperative. Shampoo is expensive, and we need to conserve, and I expect you to do your part. We have enough trouble around here, thanks to your father, without you causing problems, too."

"What does Daddy have to do with this?" I asked.

"What do you think?" Dinah said. "He doesn't send us enough money!"

I don't know what made me do it, whether it was the remark about Daddy or just everything, but I turned to Mama and said, "Then buy cheaper shampoo."

Her arm shot out from nowhere, and she smacked me across the face. Hard. So hard the shoes flew, and I lost my footing and went down on one knee.

I picked myself up and ran, streaked really, out of that room and down the stairs and out the front door, and stopped at the poplar tree and swallowed air. Great gulps of air. Tears stung my eyes, but there was as much fury in them as pain, and I did not cry. It took all of my will. Every ounce. But I did not cry.

I leaned against the tree, slid to the ground, folded my arms over my knees, and made a nest for my head. I sat there for I don't know how long—a long time—and thought black thoughts about Mama and Dinah. The sky was overcast, and the wind was up, and I was cold, but still I sat.

I wanted them to be sorry for their meanness. I'd make them sorry, if I could. I would sit there until I got pneumonia or until I froze to death. That would do it.

The only trouble was, I couldn't find a way around the problem of how I wouldn't be there to enjoy their sorrow. And I wanted that. That was the important part.

Some time later, I heard the front door, and then Dinah was there, standing over me.

"Mama said you might need these," she said. She set my shoes on the ground beside me. "And I brought your jacket. Do you want it?"

I didn't answer.

"Suit yourself," she said. She turned and walked away a few steps, then came back.

"Look, Addie, you have to understand that Mama has a lot on her mind right now."

"I know that," I said, "but does everybody have to be so awful? So mean?"

"Nobody's being mean. Mama's just very worried. We don't have enough money, and there are other things, too. Things about Daddy. We might not be able to stay in this house. You don't want to have to go live in Turlock, do you?"

"No . . ." I'd only been in Turlock once, and couldn't remember it very well. But I knew what Mama thought, and since she'd grown up there, she should know.

"Then you have to help," Dinah said.

I thought about this, and about whether I was helping, and finally I said, "I would if I knew how."

"Just help—that's all," Dinah said. "Don't waste things and don't be a problem. That would help. Can you do that?"

"I guess so," I said. "I'll try."

Dinah draped the jacket over my shoulders. "Think about coming in," she said. "It's cold out here."

And in a while I did.

And I did try to help after that. For days, weeks, I paid attention to anything that might mean waste, and counted it a real success when I managed to hang on to the same pencil all the way to Christmas vacation. I reported this to Mama, and she blinked at me for a moment like she didn't understand, but then she smiled and said, "Good."

With all the talk about money, I began to imagine a Christmas without presents under the tree. I decided I could bear this if I had to, and felt proud of my bravery. But I worried about the twins. They still believed in Santa.

Somehow Mama managed, though. Christmas came, and she cooked a turkey and sang carols with us and beamed with pleasure when we opened gifts. There weren't as many presents as before, but there were enough. I gave Mama a bottle of clear nail polish, and she went on about how it was just what she needed, and how did I know?—even though she'd suggested it herself.

Then Lord Rodhopper chose that very day to finally say, "I love you so-o-o-o much." Maybe he knew it was Christmas, or maybe he liked the slice of tangerine we gave him, or maybe it was just a coincidence. Anyhow, once he'd said it, he kept repeating it, in a high-pitched voice that sounded exactly like the twins. Mama laughed and said it was killing, and she was as near to happy that day as I'd seen her since Owen's visit.

I don't know how I made it all the way to bedtime without thinking of Daddy, but I did. And then I had a rush of fear. I wanted to leap from the bed and run downstairs and ask Mama where he was. But I knew that was wrong. Mama would get mad, and the Christmas we'd had would be spoiled.

Instead, I lay in bed and wondered to myself about Daddy. He hadn't come, hadn't called, hadn't sent so much as a card. In fact, we hadn't seen hide nor hair of him since last summer. Yet I think I believed he'd come on Christmas. Believed, without reason. So when I realized the day had passed without him, I thought he might be dead. That was what scared me. And next I thought he wasn't dead, but that maybe Dinah had told the truth and he really didn't care about us after all. This was almost more frightening than imagining he might be dead, so I stopped myself from thinking about him entirely. Just quit, flat, and went to sleep.

I love you so-o-o-o much.

Six

One day in late February Mama went to the grocery store in our car and came home in a taxi. Dinah'd gone to Jenny Cassidy's house after school that day, and Mama had left me with the twins, and she was away so long I had to go around and turn on lights.

I went out front when I heard a car in the drive, and I saw Mama with a bag of groceries, but I couldn't make sense of the taxi.

She stuck the grocery sack in my arms.

"Where's our car?" I asked.

"Just take that inside," Mama said. "Scoot."

I did, and came back for three more, and finally, when the taxi was gone, I tried again.

"Where's our car, Mama?"

"In the parking lot down by Bob's Launderette," she said. She was puling food out of the sacks and banging it down on the counter.

"Is it broken?"

"Of course it's broken. Why would I leave it there if I could have driven it home? Honestly, Adelaide! Where's Dinah?"

"At Jenny's," I said. She knew that before she left, but she must have forgotten.

"Call her," Mama said. "Tell her I need her home here right now."

Our telephone list was taped to the wall beside the phone, and it was all a jumble. I had to read each name one by one, which I was doing when Mama said, "What's taking so long, Addie?"

"I can't find the number," I said.

Mama exploded. "You're just like your father—totally useless! Do I have to do everything myself?"

She snatched up the receiver, put her finger on the number, and dialed. "It was right in front of your nose," she said.

In a minute Dinah was on the line, and Mama said, "I need you to come home and take over here for a while. That piece of junk your father left me to drive broke down today. . . . No, I don't know if it can be fixed. The man who pushed it off the street for me said something about the camshaft and pistons, and I don't know what. It may need a new engine. . . . I took a cab. . . . No, but I need to make some calls, and I can't manage all this alone, so just come home, would you?. . . Okay, that's fine. Thanks."

She hung up, then shrugged out of her coat and tossed it on the couch. "Finish putting the food away," she said. "I'll be upstairs."

I was upset—scared and mad combined. I hated the way Mama talked to me, and she did it more and more lately. It was as though she didn't like me anymore, or hardly at all.

When Dinah got home, I went up to our room

and left her to fix dinner by herself. Useless people do not help with the cooking.

As it turned out, the car was beyond repair. It needed a new engine, but the rest of the car was in such bad shape it wasn't worth the price of the engine.

Mama walked around for days with the muscles in her jaw pulsing so you could see them. She cursed Daddy regularly. "It's just like him to leave me here without a car while he cruises the western United States in a brand-new four-wheel drive!" she said. And, "I wonder how he'd like to be stuck here with four children and no transportation."

I answered the phone one evening, and Owen said, "Hi there, Cupcake, is your mama around?" He only called me Cupcake on the phone because he couldn't tell my voice from Dinah's, but still I liked it.

He and Mama talked a long time, and Mama got upset and even cried once, and said, "I don't need this now, Owen." And later she said, "And just how would that be better? Do you really think it matters whether I'm here or in Turlock with a broken car?" Then, "No. . . . Yes, but what will I do with the twins?. . . No, I don't." Then, at last, "Owen, okay. Enough. I'll think about it, okay?. . . No, I said I'd think about it, and I will, so enough, Owen, okay?"

Mama went to bed after that and stayed there for three days. If she got up to eat, I never saw her. And I don't know what she did about the twins on the first day, while Dinah and I were at school, but on the second and third days Dinah stayed home. She told me to say she was sick if anyone asked.

On the fourth day Mama got up and roamed the house in a blue-and-red-plaid bathrobe I had never laid eyes on before. Then she started talking about finding a job.

School, by now, was getting the best of me. I wasn't doing well, and I knew it. I also could not seem to help it. In class I had trouble concentrating and sometimes even found it hard to stay awake. Other times I felt as though I couldn't breathe—as though all the air had been used up. This happened whether the windows were open or not, so I can't really explain it. But I was often slightly dizzy.

The only time I was truly alert was at recess, but they don't give grades for recess, and mine were falling. Plummeting, more like. I'd started the year with *A*s and *B*s. Now I was getting *C*s, if I was lucky. And I was flat-out failing math. Mrs. Kurtz had given me a *D*, out of kindness, I suppose, or maybe she just didn't give *F*s. But if weeks and weeks go by and you never get a single problem right, you know you're failing. Nobody has to tell you.

Mrs. Kurtz spent an entire lunchtime, and then kept me after school twice, explaining the ins and outs of multiplication and division. Each time she kept me until I was absolutely sure I understood how to do it; then she let me go. And I'd turn right around and get every answer wrong the next day. I was frustrated at first, and then embarrassed—so embarrassed I hid in the girls' room all during one math test. Mrs. Kurtz never missed me, which was amazing because the entire time I was convinced I'd be found out and punished. I made up my mind to do it again.

While I floundered in room 3A, Dinah was no more than fifty yards away in 6B working her way to stardom. Her teacher, Mrs. Robbins, was supposed to be the toughest in the school, and I believed it. You could peek through the window into her classroom—which I did several times, on tiptoe, trying for a glimpse of Dinah—and every single person was sitting down working. Nobody talked. Nobody milled around. Mrs. Robbins expected work from her students, and she did not hand out praise lightly. Even in my class, kids said, "I hope I don't get Mrs. Robbins for sixth grade."

But she praised Dinah. Nearly every day she singled Dinah out for some special compliment. Which I knew, because Dinah came home and sat at the foot of the dinner table, in her chair with arms, and told us so. Mrs. Robbins read Dinah's papers aloud as an example to the class, called her to the chalkboard to demonstrate a math problem no one else could solve, or asked, "Where is Suriname?" and when three other people guessed wrong, turned to Dinah—who didn't even have her hand up!—and said, "Tell them, Dianna." And Dinah did.

Up until then, nobody in the world had called Dinah by her given name, Dianna. Then Dinah started using it herself. I saw it first on the school papers she brought to the table to show Mama. It was right up there on the top, next to the *A*s written in red. Dianna Hope Dillon. Like just plain Dinah wasn't good enough anymore.

On days when Mama had been too tense and worried to say three words to anybody, she still came alive at the dinner table listening to Dinah.

She talked about college. Dinah might go to Stanford. Maybe Harvard. She'd get a scholarship if she kept this up. And what about medical school? Had Dinah thought about becoming a doctor? Mama swelled and glowed with pride.

Dinah worked hard for every grade she got. Slaved, if necessary, and you had to admire her for it. And in a way I suppose I might have been grateful, because a Mama enthused about Dinah's future was a sight better than a Mama remote or angry.

But I was not grateful. Not even close. I found myself wishing that just once Dinah would wake up with some temporary accident of the brain that left her unable to spell a single word all day.

I wished it all the more because, in my backpack, in a small manila envelope, were my latest report card and a note to Mama from Mrs. Kurtz. I hadn't seen the note, but I'd seen the report card, and I could just imagine. I carried that envelope around for seven days straight. I did not want to give it to Mama.

In the end I had to, of course. My name was already on the chalkboard in a short list of kids who hadn't returned their signed report cards to Mrs. Kurtz. And Mama suddenly turned to me at the dinner table one evening and said, "Why is it I didn't get your report card when I got Dinah's?"

She could do that, ask a question in a way that left me completely stumped for an answer. The truth—*Because it's awful, and I'm ashamed and afraid you'll get mad*—was impossible to speak. So I stared at my plate and said nothing.

"Get it," she said.

"Now?" I said. "I could get it after dinner."

"Right this minute."

I did. My backpack was in the front hall where I'd dropped it, and I stalled out there, hoping she'd forget me. But there was an echoing silence from the family room, and I knew everyone was waiting.

I handed the envelope to Mama, slid into my seat, and pulled my napkin down into my lap. I heard Mama open the envelope, but I kept my eyes firmly on the napkin.

"Language Arts, C. Math, D," she read aloud. "Social Studies, C plus. Spelling, C minus. This is worse than the last one!"

"I know," I said.

"There is no excuse for this kind of report. None! Just what is your explanation, young lady?"

"I don't have one," I said. I twisted my napkin around a finger.

Mama opened the note from Mrs. Kurtz and read that aloud, too. " 'Addie is a well-behaved child but lacks motivation. She is frequently inattentive, and her work suffers as a result. Math is a particular problem. Please phone me to arrange a conference at your earliest convenience.' Signed, 'Emma Kurtz.' "

From the corner of my eye I could see Mama's hand drop to the table, the letter in it. And I saw the sleeve of that plaid robe. She wore it almost every day now. For a long minute she didn't say anything. Then she let loose.

"At my earliest convenience! There is nothing convenient about this, Adelaide Dillon! It's not enough that everything is going to hell in a hand basket around here, but you have to make things even harder! What could possibly be convenient about having two toddlers and no car and needing to show up at the school for a conference? Would you answer me that?"

She went right on without waiting for a reply. "Motivation, nothing! You're just lazy. You'll end up just like your father—ignorant and good-for-nothing! You don't see Dinah causing trouble around here, do you? *Do you?*"

She waited, so I knew I was supposed to answer this one. "No," I said.

"Of course not!" Mama said. "Tell me one single thing you've done lately that I might be thankful for. That *anyone* might be thankful for."

She waited again, so I thought and then said, "I got three home runs in kickball today." I didn't say it to be smart, but as soon as it was out of my mouth, I knew that was how it sounded.

Mama's arm whizzed out and she slapped me on the back of the head. Then she shoved her chair back and stood and slapped me several more times on the head and shoulders. I covered my head with my arms, but it didn't do much good.

Tiny let out a wail, and that set Bits off, and Dinah jumped up and rushed to comfort both of them.

"Go to your room!" Mama yelled. *"Get out of my sight!"*

I went.

With my clothes still on, I crawled under the spread on my side of the bed and thought tangled thoughts in the fading light. *Why did I have to catch this from Daddy? He's no good, and I'm just like him. No, that's not true. He's nice, except he doesn't care about us. I hate Mama. Hate her. I'd rather be like Daddy, even if he is good-for-*

nothing. I'm lazy. But I am motivated—Mrs. Kurtz is wrong about that. I'm very motivated—I'm just no good at school. I wonder why she wrote that? I'm so sick of Dinah. I wish she'd drop dead. I wonder why she has to do everything right.

I must have fallen asleep, because the next thing I knew it was pitch black, and a small, sticky hand was patting my face. Someone tried to stuff something cold and wet into my ear. A grape.

"You *need* your dinner," Bits's voice said. "You do."

"Bits. Tiny, are you here, too?" I reached out and snapped on the bedside lamp.

"We like you," Bits said.

"We do," Tiny said.

"I'm glad," I said. "I like you, too." I rubbed my eyes. They were in their sleepers, and Tiny had a small cluster of grapes clutched so tight in her fist that some were popped and dripping.

"You didn't finish your dinner," Bits said.

"I know, but it's okay. I wasn't all that hungry, anyway. Shouldn't you be going to bed?"

"We *were* in bed," Tiny said.

"But we got up!" Bits said.

And by then I was awake enough to understand that the twins had hatched a plot for my benefit. I sat up and ate every grape. Slowly. I *savored* each one. And then I led the twins by their sticky hands quietly back to bed.

Mama did have her conference with Mrs. Kurtz the following week, and I ran all the way home that day to stay with the twins. The whole time Mama was gone, I dreaded her return and what she would say when she got back. But she never said a word. Not one. More than once, it was on the tip of my tongue to ask about the conference, but I was afraid Mama's silence meant that truly awful things had been said. Asking might unleash another fury.

I tried harder to keep my mind on my work, but the classroom felt stuffier than ever, and a couple of times I noticed I'd quit breathing entirely, like I was holding my breath, although not on purpose. I stayed in my seat during the next math test and worked three problems I was confident of solving. On the rest, I wrote any number I thought of. I figured it was worth a chance.

As spring came on and the weather grew warmer, I took to exploring on the way home from school, until finally I discovered a trail through the canyon that came out near the bottom of Maybeck Road. It wasn't a shorter way home, but I was in no particular hurry anyhow, and the trail was more interesting. And I liked it that every day I came to know it a little better.

I spotted a dead skunk by the side of the trail and checked on it every day, watching as more and more of the skeleton was exposed to the sun. Usually I found fresh deer droppings somewhere along the way, and although I never saw a deer, I did once see a coyote. Just once, and never again. He loped across the trail far ahead, then stopped and stared right at me, frozen, then loped on. For a second I thought it was a dog, but it was a coyote, no mistake.

Once, with Daddy, in Nevada, I'd seen a coyote shot dead and hung across a barbed-wire fence. Daddy stopped the car and stared at the carcass and shook his head. "Now, I call that a crime," he said. "That poor coyote probably never in his life caught anything bigger than a jackrabbit. But try telling that to a sheep rancher. They'll shoot 'em, regardless." I don't know if he'd forgotten at that moment that Grandma and Grandpa were sheep ranchers, or that he sometimes thought to be one himself. But he felt for that coyote.

When I saw the coyote in the canyon, I thought of Daddy, and of the carcass on the fence, and wished this coyote well. I wished him food.

Toward the end of May, as I left the school grounds one afternoon, someone called out, "Hey, Addie, wait up!"

I turned, and Lizzy Siewald was chasing after me, her backpack and ponytail bouncing. She had a sideways ponytail just like her mother's, but it bounced, which was something, anyway.

"What?" I said.

"I'm coming home with you today."

"What for?" That wasn't meant to be rude, but it wasn't welcoming either. I was hoping she'd change her mind.

"My mother said to," Lizzy said. "She's taking your mom shopping today, and I'm supposed to wait at your house till they get back."

"So how come nobody told me?" I asked.

Lizzy shrugged. "Beats me."

I thought of the canyon, and my heart sank. There was no way I was taking Lizzy through the canyon, so I'd have to skip it. And just looking forward to the walk home had sustained me through the whole day of school.

I turned and continued toward home.

"Well?" Lizzy called.

I stopped again. "Well, what?"

"Well, can I walk with you? Is it okay?"

"Good grief, Lizzy. If you're coming to my house, you might as well walk with me, for pete's sake. Jeez." Leave it to Lizzy.

Lizzy was in the other third-grade class, which was a blessing, and as she walked she told me I was lucky to have Mrs. Kurtz. Which I agreed with. Then she told me Mrs. Kurtz was much easier than Mrs. Greeley, and although I had no evidence to prove it, I agreed with this, too.

"And that's lucky for you, 'cause you need it," Lizzy said.

"What's that supposed to mean?" I asked.

"It means you need an easy teacher 'cause you're almost flunking. Mom told me so."

"Great," I said. That was just great. If Lizzy knew I was having trouble in school, I wondered who didn't know. Lizzy did nothing but blab.

"Some kids are born trouble," she went on. "That's what Mom says."

"Lizzy, are you just *trying* to make me mad, or what?"

"No," she said. "Honest. I like you, really I do. I saw you kick that home run last week, the one that landed on the roof of the school—and if you *do* get kidnapped, I'll really miss you. Honest, I will."

I stopped dead in my tracks, dumbstruck for the moment.

"Lizzy Siewald, that's the most crackbrained thing I ever heard! Nobody is going to kidnap me."

"You just don't know," she said.

"You're crazy, Lizzy. You are. Just plain crazy."

"I am not!" she said. "Your father's going to

kidnap you, all four of you. And if he can't get everyone, he'll just take you. It's true!"

If I'd thought first, I never would have done what I did next. But I didn't think. I punched Lizzy. Right in the stomach. So hard she went "oooff" and sat down hard on her bottom. And then she wailed, and I guess everyone must have heard her for miles around.

Right away I knew I shouldn't have done it, but I was not sorry. Lizzy'd as good as said my father was a criminal, and that was nothing but a flat-out lie. I turned and walked away, leaving her there.

But a few doors down I could still hear her howling, and I stopped and thought it over, then went back.

"You'd better get up," I said.

Lizzy shook her head.

"Get up, Lizzy," I said. "Jeez. I'm not going to hit you again, so just get up. You can't sit there all day!"

But she didn't budge, so in a minute I hauled her to her feet and handed her her backpack.

"Just don't you ever go telling lies about my father again, Lizzy Siewald," I said. "I mean it."

"It's not a lie," she wailed.

"I'm *warning* you, Lizzy . . ."

That only made her wail louder, so I did the only other thing I could think of. I said, "Look, I'm sorry I hit you, okay? Okay?" Then I took her by the arm and steered her home.

She hollered the entire way, every step, and I apologized the entire way, mostly because I wanted her to pipe down. Which maybe is why she wouldn't stop—she may have sensed the insincerity.

Inside the house, I led her to the family room and sat her at the dining table—in Dinah's chair—and brought her cookies on a plate and a glass of milk. I apologized about six more times, until finally Lizzy was calmed down to the occasional sniffle. Then I left her there and went up to my room and sat on my bed and thought about what Mama would do when Lizzy told. Which she surely would.

I could always tell Marta's car because it had a diesel engine, and it wasn't long before I heard it in the drive. And then there was a lot of commotion downstairs with everyone coming in, and I could hear the twins and Mama and Marta and even Dinah, who must have just come in from school. I thought about going down right then, and maybe that would have been better, but I stayed put. Then Marta's car drove off.

Mama was in my room in a flash, and she had ahold of me by the hair and her face was inches from mine and she was screaming. I don't remember what all she said, except that it was about Lizzy and how Marta was her best friend, and about ingratitude, mine, and how she'd been expecting something like this from me. And one more thing, right before she let go of my hair and slapped me, about how I was going to end up in serious trouble if I thought I could go around hitting people just because I was mad.

Before the school year was over, Mama found it necessary to hit me twice more herself. And then, a few days after school ended, she packed me up and sent me away for the summer. To Turlock.

Seven

It was the last thing I expected, a summer in Turlock. And I don't know whether even Mama planned it much in advance, because she just showed up in my room early on a Sunday morning with her biggest canvas suitcase and said I should get on my feet because Owen was coming for me and there wasn't much time.

At first, I thought I was to stay with Owen. I remembered visiting him before and playing in a field with his golden retriever, Daisy. I asked Mama if she thought Owen would let Daisy sleep with me sometimes, and then she said I'd be staying with Grandma and Grandpa, not Owen, and that I was to mind them and not give them any trouble or make her ashamed of me. And she said I should pack some things to keep myself amused so I wouldn't be underfoot all the time. I picked out a pack of cards and my Frisbee, and an old ViewMaster with slides, and my yo-yo and one of those little games where you try to shake the beads into holes.

I didn't know whether to be excited or frightened, really. I felt like I must be pretty grown-up to go off for the whole summer, and I hadn't seen Grandma and Grandpa Canby for ages and ages, so I looked forward to that. But I'd never been away from my family for longer than overnight, and that scared me some. I wished the twins or Dinah were coming, too. And then there was Turlock.

"Why am I going alone?" I asked. "Can't Dinah come with me?"

Mama was chucking clothes into the suitcase in a hurry, and she didn't even slow down when she answered. "Your grandparents are too old to look after more than one child, Adelaide. And anyway, I need Dinah here to take care of the twins. I'm starting work next week, and I can't keep track of all four of you this summer and work, too. So someone needs to go."

"But I can keep track of myself," I said.

"No," Mama said. Just that. *No.*

Owen arrived while I was still matching socks retrieved from the clean laundry, and Mama left me to finish the packing and ran downstairs to make coffee.

I got my toothbrush from the bathroom, and then, without knowing just why, I took the two photos and the Wellington Motors pen from under the dresser drawer and stuck them in the suitcase, on the bottom. Then I zipped the suitcase and bumped it down the stairs.

Owen drank just one cup of coffee—gulped it, almost, and never took his hat off—then Mama told me for the fifth time to behave myself and Owen said next time he'd try to come for a real visit. Then, so fast it was a blur, we were in the pickup and gone.

It hit me about halfway across the San Mateo Bridge that I wouldn't be back for a long time, and I couldn't remember if I'd actually said good-bye to the twins, and I don't know what else, and I just started to bawl.

Owen said, "Are you going to be okay, Addie? Do you want me to take you back?"

I heaved a huge sob and said yes, I did. And Owen said just to hang on a few minutes because he couldn't turn on the bridge and we'd have to get to the toll plaza first. But by the time we got there, I'd had time to think what Mama would say if Owen came driving me home because of my blubbering, and I told him never mind.

"You sure?" he said.

I nodded. "Yes."

"Well, I'll tell you what," he said. "I'm hungry, so I think we'll stop for breakfast up ahead if that's okay with you. And if you change your mind before we're done with breakfast, I'll take you back. How's that?"

I said, "Okay." But I didn't change my mind. I knew there was no going back. Not really.

I ordered way too much food, and Owen had to finish my pancakes for me, and then we were off again.

We went over the Altamont Pass, which I recognized because it is lined with windmills—hundreds of them—running along the hillsides. I'd been on this road before, on the way to Nevada, but never when the wind was blowing so hard. Nearly every windmill was turning, and it was eerie and beautiful all at the same time. It made me almost woozy to watch.

Later, when I saw a sign for Tracy, I asked Owen if I could turn on the radio, and he said, "Help yourself."

I fiddled with the dial until I found Emmylou Harris singing "Save the Last Dance for Me," and I knew I had what I wanted and settled back.

Owen laughed and said, "So you really are a chip off the old block, after all."

I knew he meant Daddy, so I said, "Maybe," and turned and looked out the window on my right.

Owen reached over and took hold of my arm and gave it a squeeze. "It's okay," he said. "I'm not big on taking sides when people get divorced."

I thought about that for a minute, then asked, "Did you ever want to have kids, Owen?"

"All the time," Owen said, "all the time. Maybe I will yet one day—who knows?"

It stuck with me, the way he said "all the time," and when another mile or two had passed, I said, "If you did have kids and you got divorced, would you want to visit them?"

"You bet!" Owen said.

"That's what I thought," I said.

I don't know whether it was the music on the radio or talking with Owen, but I felt all right after that. Not happy or sad, just all right.

We got to Turlock in no time at all, and I partly recognized Grandma and Grandpa's house and partly didn't. It was a one-story green stucco, and maybe it had been pink before—I wasn't sure. But Grandma and Grandpa looked the same, except Grandpa Canby had a cane.

Owen said he had a job to get to and didn't even stay for coffee this time—just carried my suitcase in for me and said good-bye. And there I was.

I think if I'd known that morning what it would mean to spend a summer in Turlock, I never would have climbed into that truck with Owen in the first place. Wild horses couldn't have dragged me from the house.

It wasn't Turlock itself I minded. Turlock was nice, really, or what I saw of it. It was flat, and sometimes blazing hot, but mostly it was just a nice, small town with kids riding bicycles and storekeepers who asked your name. Only I didn't see much of Turlock, because Grandma and Grandpa had it in their heads that I shouldn't be let out of their sight. And that was the trouble.

Their house had seven rooms, and I got the pick of the two guest bedrooms and chose the one that had been Mama's when she was a girl. It looked out on the backyard, which had three fruit trees and was otherwise planted, border to border, with vegetables and flowers. Grandpa worked out there in the early mornings, and sometimes I went with him and helped water or carried tools or else just watched. I had to mind where I stepped. There was barely an inch where something fragile wasn't growing.

The other rooms in the house were crammed, every one of them, with Grandma's collection of antique china and porcelain figurines, and Grandpa's collection of everything else—magazines, tools, stamps, old electric motors connected to nothing. And I wasn't to touch any of it, which would have mattered more if any of it had been interesting to me, which it wasn't.

They had enough sagging furniture to fill a secondhand shop. I imagined that, when a piece of furniture wore out, they simply shoved it aside to make room for something else. And it was impossible to believe that any of it had ever been new.

That's the house I spent the summer in. Grandma cooked and cleaned and watched soap operas. Grandpa gardened and puttered and watched baseball. They both watched game shows and the evening news. They did not go out. Not if they could help it. Grandma was bothered by the heat, and Grandpa was bothered by his knee, so they stayed in and ran the air conditioner all day and all night.

And because I was not allowed out of their sight, I stayed in, too. Turlock was sunny. The sun shone every single day, bar none, all day long, all summer long. And I stayed in, and watched through the window. From time to time some kids would pass, on the way to somewhere, and I began to wish I had a bicycle. I would climb on it and go racing after them and ask to join in whatever it was they were doing.

But when I asked Grandma and Grandpa for permission to play outside, just to find someone to toss my Frisbee with me, they always said no. It was too dangerous.

I thought about that—pondered it, truly—and looked out the windows and tried to see the danger. But I couldn't. I couldn't see it, and they didn't explain it.

Sometimes Owen came. Owen! He came in his battered Stetson like a rescuing angel and carted me off for the day. Twice we went to his place, and I played with Daisy in the field while Owen pulled rotting boards from his back porch and replaced them with new ones. Daisy was getting old, but she still liked to fetch a ball, and I'd swear she remembered me, and Owen said I was probably right.

Owen drove me to Merced one afternoon to a barbeque and square dance, and I danced until my knees got wobbly and I nearly was good at it. Once in a while, if he happened to be passing, Owen would stop in and ask if I wanted to ride with him while he went to talk business with a farmer. I always said yes.

One afternoon we stopped at a place near the Merced River, and I left Own talking and wandered down to the riverbank alone. I got engrossed there, skipping rocks across the water with the sun beating down on my head, and completely forgot about the time. I was gone I don't know how long before I realized Owen had said he'd be just a few minutes and it was way past a few. It was closer to an hour. I tore all the way back to where he'd left the pickup truck parked in the shade, and there was Owen—stretched out on the front seat with his hat over his face and his boots hanging out the open door.

"I forget the time," I said, breathing hard. "I'm sorry, Owen, really."

He lifted his hat and squinted at me from one eye. "Do I look unhappy?" he asked. "I knew you'd be back sooner or later."

If Owen had never done another thing in his life, I think I would love him still, just for that one hour. For the delicious feeling of knowing that I could go away and then that I could come back, and that both the going and the coming were okay.

But I saw Owen only ten or a dozen times all summer. The rest of the time I spent in my grandparents' house, playing endless games of solitaire, building card houses, and wandering from room to room looking out windows. Restlessness grew in me until it became an agony, and I begged for escape. But the answer was always no.

Day after day, I made elaborate plots to run away. In my mind, I followed each scheme, step by step, like you'd follow a string to find its end. But sooner or later they all landed me in the same place—face-to-face with Mama. And she'd be furious. Running away would not be her idea of behaving.

At night I looked forward to bed, because I could close the door on the air conditioning and turn out the light and open the window and fall asleep to the sound of crickets. And I knew then I would dream. I learned to snatch the dreams in the mornings before they disappeared and have little bits all over again. All of my dreams that summer took place outside.

Occasionally, Mama telephoned. But always when I was asleep. Grandma would say the next day, "I talked to your mama last night. She misses you."

If she missed me so much, I didn't know why she couldn't phone when I was awake and tell me so herself. I thought about that, and when I thought she might be due to call again, I went to bed with the door open and the window closed and kept myself awake and listened for the phone to ring. I did that for several nights running. I planned to go out front and speak to her when she phoned. She could tell me she missed me, and I would tell her I was homesick and wanted to come home and wouldn't be any trouble to keep track of. And she'd say, "Yes, okay, come home right away."

Finally, one night the telephone did ring late, and I listened until I was sure it must be Mama, then jumped out of bed and ran all the way down the hall. But Grandma hung up as I got to the front room.

"Was that Mama?" I asked.

"Why, yes, Addie, it was." Grandma looked surprised to see me. "What are you doing up?"

"I wanted to speak to her," I said.

"Goodness, I had no idea you were still awake," Grandma said.

"Can we call her back?" I asked. "Right now?"

"We could," Grandma said. "Or maybe you could write to her tomorrow. Was there something special you wanted to say?"

"I wanted to tell her how I am."

"Oh, well . . . that's all right then," Grandma said. "I told her myself. I told her you're no trouble at all and that you're doing fine."

"But I'm *not* doing fine! I'm doing terrible! There's nothing to do here and you won't even let me out on the sidewalk! *It's just like being in jail!*" I ended by screaming, and tears poured down my face, but I didn't care. I just stood there and let them.

"Now!" Grandma said. "Now, now. You don't want to get worked up, Adelaide."

Grandpa shoved himself out of his chair. "She already is worked up," he said. "I expect we need some of that chocolate cake."

"I don't need cake! I need to go home!"

But he went out to the kitchen, anyway, and Grandma came over and steered me into an overstuffed chair. "You can't go home yet, Adelaide. Your mother needs you to stay here. You'd just worry her if you told her you wanted to go home. And you must believe me—anything we tell you to do is for your own good."

"How?" I asked. "How is it good to be homesick? Did Mama say that?"

"That's not what I mean," Grandma said. She handed me a tissue. "Now blow," she said. "And when you're settled down, we'll talk about this."

I blew. "I'm settled down now," I said. I wasn't, but if Grandma was going to explain how all of this was good for me, I did not intend to wait.

Grandma eased into the chair next to mine and fiddled with the fringe on the arm for a minute. Then she said, "We don't want to make you unhappy, Addie. But it's really not safe for you to play outside."

"Why?" I asked. "Other kids play outside. I see them all the time."

"Other children aren't you," she said.

"But *why?*"

Grandpa returned carrying a slice of cake and a glass of milk. "I think it's best to tell her," he said.

"Now you hush," Grandma said to him.

"Tell me *what?*" I said.

"You can't keep a thing like this a secret forever," Grandpa said. He set the cake and milk on a table near me.

"A thing like *what?*" I demanded.

Grandma sighed. Then she sighed again. "All right," she said. "I suppose you're right." She reached over and took both my hands in hers, then said, "Adelaide, your father may have plans to take you. And if you're safe inside with us, why then . . ."

I pulled my hands free. "You mean kidnap me," I said. Of course. I knew it all along. Not in my conscious mind, but deep in my bones, I knew what was going on all along. My father. *Daddy.*

"Well . . ." Grandpa said.

"It's not true," I said.

"Now, Addie, your mama has reason to believe—"

"I don't care!" I said. "She's wrong. If she thinks that, she's wrong. Everybody's wrong!"

"Now, Adelaide—"

"It's a big, fat lie!" I said. "And you can keep me in this house for the rest of the summer if you like, but I still won't believe it. You can't make me believe my father is a kidnapper!"

I ran back to my room and slammed the door. Twice, because the first time it bounced and didn't catch. And I opened my window and crawled into bed and listened to the crickets. And thought about my father.

I thought about where he might be right then, and what he'd think if he knew everybody thought he was a kidnapper. He'd be pretty mad, I guessed. If it wasn't true, he'd be sure to be mad.

If it wasn't true.

That's when the first doubt crept in. I told myself that everyone was wrong, but all of a sudden I had this doubt. *What if they're right? What if he does plan to kidnap me? Does he even know where I am?*

Right then, and for the first time in my life, I

was afraid of my father. *Daddy.* The fear came and went like a sudden shiver, and I did not like it.

I snapped on the light and got up and pulled the suitcase from under the bed where it had been since I'd arrived. I unzipped it and took out the picture of me and Daddy. And then the picture of me on Damnhorse. Click. I could see him. And he was smiling, and he wasn't someone to be afraid of. Not in the least.

I studied the photos for quite a while. Then I put them back and got back in bed and turned off the light and listened to the crickets again. Then I had another thought.

If he does come to get me, maybe I'll just go.

For the rest of the summer, except when Owen came, I roamed the house and stared out the windows. Only now it was different. Now I had something to watch for. I didn't tell a soul, but all the time I looked out the windows, I watched for Daddy. Watched and hoped.

I kept a piece of paper on my bureau, and each night at bedtime I made a mark for that day. I counted the marks every night, and sometimes several times a day, but their number never seemed to grow. Each day lasted forever, and all the days together lasted a lifetime. Time stood absolutely still.

And yet a day did come when I counted sixty-seven marks. And on that day, at long last, Owen took me home.

Eight

Sometimes, without meaning to, you change, and you don't even know about it until it's all over and done with and too late to turn back. Even then, you may not know about it until someone else points it out. And I think that's what happened to me that summer. I went away, and when I came back I had changed. I was glad to be home. Relieved, truly relieved. But if someone had asked me if I felt like I belonged there anymore, I'd have had to say no.

Dinah noticed the change first, long before I did. She seemed happy to see me, and I was happy to see her, and I'd been home about three hours and we were standing in our room when she said, "You're different, Addie." Just like that.

"It's not me—it's this room," I said.

And I thought it was. The room had been completely redone, and I wasn't sure I cared for the transformation. The double bed was gone. It wasn't in the twins' room—it was just gone. Dinah and I had single beds, and they were on opposite sides of the room, against the walls. About as far apart as you can get.

The beds were covered with rose-patterned spreads, reversible, with a white background on one side and blue on the other. And beside each bed on the hardwood floor was a small throw rug.

"Do you like it?" Dinah asked.

"I'm not used to it yet," I said.

"You don't have to be used to it to know if you like it, Addie. Come on."

My suitcase was open on my bed, and I sat down next to it. "Maybe plain would have been better," I said.

"Plain spreads, you mean?"

"Yeah."

"What's wrong with these?" she asked.

"I don't know," I said. "Maybe they're okay. Maybe when I get used to them, I'll like them better. I don't know."

Dinah looked back and forth between the beds. "Well, I like them," she said. "I picked them out."

I shrugged. "It doesn't really matter, Dinah. They're okay."

"You *are* different, Addie. I swear you are."

"Well, I know I'm taller," I said. "Mama already told me that about six times." I pulled a stack of underwear from the suitcase and set it on the bed.

"Do you want me to help you unpack?" Dinah asked.

I considered that. It didn't look like much to do, really. And then there were those photos and the pen.

"I guess not," I said. "Thanks, but I don't think I really need help."

Dinah went downstairs then to help Mama with dinner, and I finished the unpacking, then tested the bed some, and looked around the room and tried to figure out why it looked so small. Which is when I noticed the brush and hand mirror on Dinah's dresser. They were a matched set, antique, with sterling silver backs, and I recognized them because they'd been on Mama's dresser for years. They were her pride and joy, handed down to Mama from her great-grandmother. Now, it seemed, they belonged to Dinah. I pulled the door closed behind me and went downstairs myself.

Mama was at the stove, and Dinah was peeling a cucumber into the sink. Grandpa had loaded me with vegetables when I left, so I knew salad was on the menu.

Mama exclaimed again at how much I'd grown.

"I know, Mama," I said.

She was making burritos—as a special treat in my honor, she said, although we all liked them—and she left the beef sizzling in the pan and came and stood in front of me.

"Look," she said. "You're up to my chin."

Without thinking, I stepped back. "I know, Mama," I said again.

Something was wrong. Ever since I'd walked in the door from Turlock, I'd been having trouble saying "Mama." The word stuck in my throat. I didn't know what to make of this, and I began to feel fidgety. At any moment I expected someone to remark on how I stumbled over Mama's name.

I offered to grate the cheese, and went at it hard, grateful for a way to cover my awkwardness.

"Tell us about your summer," Mama said. She said it brightly, the same way you'd ask someone to tell you about a day at Santa Cruz boardwalk. And that bothered me. Didn't she *know?*

I took a deep breath. "What do you call your mother?" I asked.

"Grandma?" she said. She sounded surprised.

"Yes," I said. "What do you call her when you don't call her Grandma?"

Mama furrowed her brow. "Why, Mom, I guess. Why do you ask?"

"Because I was wondering if I could call you something besides Mama," I said. "Like maybe Mom."

"Well . . ."

"I *told* you she was different," Dinah said.

"I suppose," Mama said. Then she added quickly, "But not Mom, Addie. Anything but Mom."

"How about Mother then," I asked.

"Mother!" Dinah said. "Why would you want to call her Mother?"

"I guess I've just outgrown Mama," I said. I transferred the grated cheese into the bowl and waited for Mama's answer.

At last she said, "Mother is fine." She didn't sound happy about it, but she wasn't exactly mad either. And for some reason I felt oddly relieved.

Dinah ran water into the sink and rinsed the lettuce and handed it to me to tear, and Mother sliced the beef into thin strips. Then she said again, "So tell us about your summer, Addie. Tell us what you liked best."

"Coming home," I said.

Mother laughed as though I'd made a joke, but Dinah shot me a warning look.

"I'm sure you did something you liked in Turlock," Mother said.

I thought for a long time, then said, "I went to a square dance once with Owen. But that was in Merced."

"Good!" Mother said.

"Oh, lucky," Dinah said.

"You think I'm lucky?" I was truly astonished.

"At least you weren't cooped up here all summer minding the twins and cleaning house," Dinah said. "I'd have loved to go square dancing with Owen!"

I looked over to where the twins sat on the family-room couch. They were playing some whispering game with two rag dolls I'd never seen before. Except for when I'd first arrived, they had completely ignored me. I felt bad about that.

"The twins aren't any trouble to mind," I said.

"Still . . ." Dinah said.

"Dinah worked very hard this summer," Mother declared. "I don't know what I'd have done without her."

I didn't know what I was supposed to say to that, so I said nothing. In fact, I couldn't think of anything much to say during dinner either. And I wasn't even really hungry, although the burritos were good.

It didn't make sense. There I was, home, where I'd yearned to be for so long a time, and somehow nothing was the way I'd pictured it. I decided I was tired, and went to bed before anyone. Even the twins.

Mother was up early the next day and in a dress for work. It was strange to see her head out the door in her running shoes, with her high heels and a lunch in a bag over her shoulder. I knew she had to walk down to the highway to catch a bus, and I watched her until she was out of sight around the bend.

I knew what I wanted to do next. I pulled on jeans and a shirt and knocked on the door to the twins' room.

"Come in," someone called.

I let myself in. Both twins were in Bits's bed, and each clutched a rag doll to her chest.

"Hi, you two," I said.

Tiny thrust her doll into the air and said, "Hi, Addie. I'm Miss Tinsel Toes." She wiggled the doll to show who was speaking.

I sat on the foot of the bed. It was a pretty rag doll with blond yarn hair and a red gingham dress. No tinsel on its toes, but never mind. Bits's doll was nearly identical, but with red yarn hair and a blue gingham dress.

"I like your dolls," I said.

Bits thrust her doll forward. "We like you, too, Addie. I'm Miss Bows and Bows." She pronounced it 'bows' as in bowing before an audience, and 'bows' as in bows in your hair.

"Miss Bows and Bows?" I said.

"Yes," the doll answered. "But you can call me Bowsie for short. Do you think I'm pretty?"

"I do," I said. "I was just thinking that. How do you do, Bowsie?" I shook the doll's hand.

"And you can call me Tansy for short," Tiny's doll said.

"How do you do, Tansy?" I shook that doll's hand, too. It seemed the thing to do.

"Let me outta here!" a deep voice called.

"Lord Rodhopper!" I'd forgotten. I went to the

cage and pulled the cover off and said hello to him as well. His cage was dirty, I noticed, and I thought maybe I'd help the twins change it later on.

"If you two will get dressed and have your cereal, I'll take you for a wagon ride," I said.

The twins went into a whispering charade with the dolls and then Bits stuck her doll out. "Bits says okay," Bowsie said. "She says you give good rides."

"Tiny says okay, too," Tansy said.

If someone had just explained it to me right off, it wouldn't have taken me half the day to catch on. But I found out you could not talk to the twins directly anymore. Period. If you wanted to do business with Tiny and Bits, you did it through their dolls or not at all. The twins were not available.

It was cute for the fist half hour, but then it began to wear on me. At the breakfast table, I said, "Could you two quit this and just be yourselves for a while?"

"What's she talking about?" Tansy said.

"She's been away," Bowsie said solemnly. "She doesn't know yet that we're real. But don't worry. She'll like us as much as the twins when she knows."

"She may like us better!" Tansy said.

"She may!" Bowsie agreed.

I groaned. "I doubt it," I said.

I considered canceling the wagon ride, and said so. When I'd thought of it, I'd wanted to take the twins, not a couple of spooky dolls who thought they were real. But if I hoped to pressure Tiny and Bits into coming back to reality, I was wasting my time. They were content with where they were.

I stalled around for quite a while, but finally gave in when Tansy said, "We *have* to go. Tiny says she really missed your rides."

Dinah stopped us as we were about to go out the back door. She said if I was thinking of taking the twins in the wagon, I'd have to forget it.

"You can play in the back," she said, "but not out front. And you can't leave our property."

"Who says?" I asked.

"Mama does. She wants everyone indoors or in the backyard at all times. So she'll know where we are."

"She didn't tell *me* that," I said.

"I'm telling you," Dinah said. "You're supposed to mind me, Addie."

I knew what she was driving at, of course. And I also thought it was cuckoo. Mother couldn't really mean to keep us all locked up forever.

"I've taken the twins on lots of wagon rides, and Mother never cared before. So I'm going," I said. "If she doesn't like it, she can tell me so herself."

Bits held up her doll. "Hooray for Addie!" she said. "Dinah wants to be the boss, and Addie won't let her!"

"Stay out of this, Bits," Dinah said.

"I'm not Bits!" the doll said. "I'm Bowsie. Bits didn't say anything."

"Let's go," I said, and pushed the back door open. The twins followed.

"I'm telling," Dinah called after me.

"So tell," I said. "That suits me fine!"

I loaded the four of them in the wagon and headed off down the hill. I crossed Maybeck at Arroyo and turned north, and after a while the pleasure of simply walking around took my mind off Dinah and the extra passengers in the wagon. I just walked and smelled the air and was glad to be home.

So I was startled when I reached an intersection with a sign that read Westfall Way, and a voice from the wagon said, "Don't turn here. That's how you got lost last summer."

I turned sharply around. "I never told you I was lost!" I said.

"But you *were,*" Tansy said.

"Don't worry, though," Bowsie said. "The twins don't know. *We* know, but the twins don't."

"They don't know *every*thing," Tansy said.

I plunked myself down on the parking strip and just rested my head in my hands. I was completely at sea now. I didn't know what to make of the dolls.

"We won't tell," Bowsie said. "You don't have to be scared, Addie, because we'll never tell."

I started to say I wasn't scared, but then I realized maybe I was. "What *else* do you know?" I asked.

"We know you didn't like it in Turlock," Tansy said. "We knew that all summer."

"And we know you don't like Mama much anymore," Bowsie said.

"But I *do,*" I said.

"No, you don't," Tansy said. "But that's okay. We don't like her much either."

"Or Dinah," Bowsie said. "Dinah is way too bossy."

"But the *twins* like her," Tansy said hastily.

"Oh, yes!" Bowsie agreed. "The twins *love*

Mama and Dinah. They love them a lot. Only we don't."

And that's the way it was. It took some getting used to, but after a time even I had spells when I forgot the dolls weren't real. They went everywhere with the twins—and Miss Tinsel Toes and Miss Bows and Bows were forces to be reckoned with. They *knew* things. And they spoke the truth with . . . eerie recklessness. They also had opinions. The twins didn't, but the dolls did. I think I'd have feared the dolls if they hadn't been my friends.

I missed Tiny and Bits, but I came to like the dolls. Not better. Never better. But nearly as much.

I did get in trouble over the wagon ride, of course. Mother pointed out that I'd been home less than twenty-four hours and was already creating problems. She was serious about keeping us under lock and key and did not want to be questioned. And Dinah was to be obeyed. If she gave an order, I could either follow it or take my chances with Mother.

Dinah went to middle school that year, and the twins started kindergarten. It was my job to walk them to school. Which I didn't mind except that they were in no particular hurry to get there. They liked school, or so Tansy and Bowsie reported, but they liked a leisurely stroll even better. And no matter how early we started, we always arrived late. They would not be rushed. My teacher got fed up and sent home about half a dozen notes before Mother finally phoned her and explained.

The twins and their dolls were a curiosity to the other kids at school, and for a while I enjoyed celebrity status as their sister. Kids came to me to find out which twin was which, and they were alternately described as adorable and weird.

"Are they like that at home?" Jody Masters asked.

"Yes," I said with pride. "They're always like that."

Mother paid an elderly lady named Mrs. Ivey to pick the twins up after school and keep them until dinnertime. She was less like day care than like a foster grandparent, and I believe she truly loved the twins. She baked cookies and did paper-and-glue projects with them. Mrs. Ivey even passed muster with Tansy and Bowsie, who were no push-overs.

Dinah was busier in seventh grade than she'd ever been before. She joined the science club, which met after school on Tuesdays, and she had a slew of new friends who sometimes came home with her in twos and threes. She ran for class vice-president and won. She was always working on something. She sweated over her homework late into the night, and after school if she didn't have some meeting she often stopped by the grocery store on the way home to save Mother a trip. She'd puff into the house loaded down with books and food, and then not even stop to catch her breath before she ran the vacuum around the family room or threw a load of laundry in the washer. As often as not, she'd start dinner. And if there was time, she even ran outside and cut flowers for the dining table.

Dinah slaved. And she did it all for Mother. "If this house is clean when Mama gets home, she'll be in a better mood," Dinah said.

I had permanent dish duty already, and something in me did not like to take orders from Dinah, so sometimes I helped and sometimes I didn't, depending on how she asked and whether I was sick of her on a particular day.

Anyway, I disbelieved the idea that a clean house improved Mother's mood. Her mood seemed the same as always to me. Crummy. And she was usually mad at me whether I helped Dinah or not. It didn't improve my situation that I did as poorly in fourth grade as I had in third, and Mother told me regularly that I was headed straight for trouble. I believed her.

I walked home from school through the canyon every chance I got. The canyon was a secret I kept to myself, out of some feeling that if Mother and Dinah knew they'd find a reason to tell me not to walk there. And I did not want that.

I ate lunch with Jody Masters most days that year, and one day when she let me ride her new bike around the playground after school, I told her about the canyon trail. Then the next day I took her there. I was glad I did. She noticed the things I liked, and she didn't say anything dumb like, "Oh, gross," when I showed her the skunk skeleton. It was all bones now, and even some of those had disappeared, but Jody said she could tell it was a skunk from the teeth.

I liked Jody more the better I got to know her, and one day when we'd walked through the canyon together, I invited her home. She was as interested in our house as she was in the canyon, and I even showed her Daddy's old study and took her up to the twins' room and introduced her to Lord Rodhopper. He said, "I love you so-o-o-o much," and hopped around his cage like he was showing off.

Jody was fascinated by the twins' room, where there were two of every toy. And I guess that would seem unusual if you didn't have twins in your own family.

She noticed that one of their beds was neatly made and covered with toys, while the other was still rumpled from nighttime. "Why do they have two beds if they only sleep in one?" she asked. And I had to tell her the truth, which was that they'd only been sleeping together since last summer, and I didn't know why. There was a lot about the twins I didn't know.

That's when Dinah came home and found us.

"What are you doing in here?" she asked.

"I'm showing Jody the twins' room and Lord Rodhopper," I said. "This is Jody Masters."

"Hi," Jody said.

Dinah said, "I remember you from grade school." Then she turned to me and said, "You're not allowed to have company."

My cheeks flushed hot. "Why not?" I asked.

"Because it's not responsible to have kids in the house when no grown-ups are home," she said.

"*You* do," I said.

"That's different," Dinah said. "I'm older, and anyhow everyone knows I'm dependable. You're not. Ask Mama if you want to know."

"We're not doing anything wrong!" I said. "And you are not in charge of me!"

"That's okay," Jody said. "I have to go, anyway." She edged past Dinah and out the door.

I followed Jody down the stairs and to the front door. I think I mumbled something about being sorry, but I was so mortified I'm not exactly sure what I said.

The next morning at school, I avoided Jody. I was ashamed and embarrassed and just did not know what to say to her. But at lunchtime she came and joined me in our usual place.

She pulled an apple from her bag and rubbed it on her sleeve. "Your sister's really something," she said.

"Yeah," I said. I fumbled longer than necessary in my lunch bag.

"Well, if she was my sister, I wouldn't let her get away with acting like that. I'd poison her soup or something."

I felt a flush creep up my neck. "She's really not always that way."

"Still . . ." Jody crunched firmly into the apple.

"Still," I agreed.

Still. A heavy awkwardness fell between us, and from that day, Jody and I were never really friends again. We were friendly . . . but not quite friends. I can't explain it any better than that.

Mother backed Dinah up, of course. I was not responsible enough to have guests in the house unless Mother was home. She told me this in a long lecture delivered in the family room, during which she mentioned my grades and where I left my jacket and how many times she'd had to remind me about the dishes in the past month.

Tiny and Bits stood by all the while, watching. Then, as Mother was winding down, Bits held up her doll and said, "I don't think that's fair, Tansy, do you?"

"No-o-o-o," Tansy said. "It's very unfair. That's what I think."

Mother pointed a finger at the twins. "Tiny and Bits! When I want your opinion, I'll ask for it. Understood?"'

"The twins didn't say *anything,*" Bowsie said. "*We* did. The twins agree with you, Mama. They think you're *very* fair."

"Only *we* don't," Tansy said.

Mama pointed again and opened her mouth. Then she snapped it shut without a word and left the room.

The twins looked absolutely serene.

The next time Dinah asked me to help clean the house to please Mother, I just flat out said no. If Dinah wanted to work herself half to death to make Mother happy, let her—she was the one who got the thanks and such privileges as Mother handed out. She could do the work. I would not.

I still did the dishes and whatever else was needed to save my own skin—which was sometimes at risk because Mother backed up her orders with an open palm. But except for that, I kept out of the way.

All that year and into the next I wondered about Daddy. Wondered and watched and waited. And sometimes I got pretty mad at him, to tell the truth. Hadn't he said he would get a place to live where we could come to visit? Hadn't he *promised?* Well, maybe not promised, but almost. Didn't he care about us at all? Didn't he care about *me?* How could he just leave me here?

Maybe he'd changed his mind. Where had he gone to, anyway? I kept thinking about Nevada, and about sheep, and wondering if he'd become a rancher. Or maybe he was no place in particular. Maybe he was just out there somewhere, roaming, bouncing along over the desert like a tumbleweed with no real destination.

When the phone rang, I listened in case it was Daddy. It never was. With fading hope, I watched for him out the front windows. On the way to and from school, I inspected every passing car. I looked for him everywhere, and he did not come. And I decided, finally, that if Daddy had ever really meant to kidnap me, he was not trying very hard.

Nine

Two months to the day after the twins turned seven, Lord Rodhopper died. They came in one late afternoon from Mrs. Ivey's and found him, cold and stiff on the floor of his cage. And, oh, the sorrow. Tiny and Bits clung to each other and wept, streams and rivers and oceans of tears. They wept with a helplessness that tore at your heart. They wept and could not be consoled.

They blamed themselves for Lord Rodhopper's death, and that was the worst of all. They could not be persuaded they weren't somehow at fault.

"If only we hadn't gone to school," Tiny said.

"If only we'd come home instead of going to Mrs. Ivey's," Bits said.

"Maybe we didn't feed him enough."

"Maybe we didn't clean his cage enough."

"Maybe he didn't know how much we loved him," they said.

Dinah said, "He had a good life. Sometimes birds just die."

"Not Lord Rodhopper!" Tiny sobbed.

"Oh, Lord Rodhopper," Bits whispered, "we did not want you to die."

Mother searched for a cookie tin of suitable shape and size. The twins chose one with a sleigh on the top and garlands of popcorn and cranberries around the sides. It was clearly meant for Christmas cookies, but Tiny and Bits were satisfied. Lord Rodhopper would need to eat, they pointed out, and cranberries and popcorn would make him happy. Mother found a scrap of rich, green brocade to line the tin, and Dinah and I donated a long, floral scarf from our costume collection. Tiny and Bits wound Lord Rodhopper in the scarf and gently laid him down.

But when Mother dug a hole under the lilac bush, the twins balked. They would not put him in the ground. Even in his floral scarf and brocade-lined tin, he might be cold. And he wouldn't like it in the ground, they said. Birds liked to hop and fly. How could Lord Rodhopper do those things in the ground?

They opened the tin and unwound the scarf and found out he was dead all over again. And they wept all over again. But they would not bury him.

It took two days and a great deal of persuading before a funeral was held. All the dolls attended. The rag dolls were still very real, but there were Barbie dolls now, too, and others, and they sometimes talked as well. But not on this day. The twins managed this occasion entirely on their own. The dolls sat in respectful silence around the grave.

It was a majestic funeral. Our yard was stripped of flowers to lay over the grave, and even Mrs. Ivey, who had never met Lord Rodhopper, came with a handful of chrysanthemums. Tiny held the tin coffin while Bits read a letter they had composed all by themselves.

"Dear Lord Rodhopper," she read. "We are very sad you died. Please come back. We love you so much."

She folded the letter in a square and put it in the tin with Lord Rodhopper. Then they knelt and placed the tin in the ground and scooped the dirt in by hand.

Tiny and Bits kept Lord Rodhopper's cage in their room, but when Owen wrote and offered to find them another bird, they said no. I often passed by the open door of their room and saw them in quiet communion in front of the cage. The cage was clean, the seed and water dishes full, and the twins whispered and kept watch.

They dug Lord Rodhopper up. They dug him up and unwound him and saw that he was still dead, and wept fresh tears. Then they reburied him.

Mother found them at it and said, "Don't do that again. He'd dead. Dead birds are germy."

But the twins crept out when she wasn't looking and dug him up a second and third time. I saw them out there, kneeling on the ground. I saw the floral scarf unwound and Tiny and Bits nodding as though satisfied of something. Then they put him back.

Mother caught them at it the fourth time around, and that night, when the twins were in bed asleep, she took a shovel and moved the grave, ending, as she said, all future disinterments.

I was in Mrs. Robbin's sixth grade class that year, which may have caused her as much unhappiness as it did me. She had high hopes for me, which I at least did not, and during the first weeks of school I saw her disappointment grow until finally she looked at me and sadly shook her head.

I read her mind. *I cannot believe you are the sister of Dianna Hope Dillon.*

Mother no longer bothered to lecture me on my report cards. But neither would she sign them. She glanced at them, then left them on the dining table day after day as though they were simply not worthy of her attention. Each report period, my name ended up alone on the chalkboard, the last person whose card had not been returned. I wondered if my classmates could read the invisible subscript. Adelaide Dillon *whose report card is so awful it's not worth signing.*

Dinah sat at the dinner table, in her chair with arms, and told me I'd have to work harder in math if I was to get into Algebra in ninth grade. "Really, Addie," she said. "You just don't try. You don't really work at anything. I don't know what's wrong with you."

I didn't know what was wrong with me either. But I did know I wished Dinah would keep her mouth shut sometimes.

"We can't all be as perfect as you, Dinah," I said.

"Well, I was just trying to help," she said. "There's no need to be rude."

"Oh, am I being rude, too? I'm so sorry. Here, let me make it up to you. Let me kiss your hand."

Tiny giggled and Bits said, "Uh-oh."

Dinah said, "Tell her to stop, Mama. She'll just keep it up if you don't tell her to stop."

"Addie, if you can't behave, go to your room," Mother said.

I put my napkin on the table. "Certainly," I said. "I wouldn't want to upset Dinah." And I went.

I knew about unpleasant, disagreeable children, and I knew that I was one. I *felt* disagreeable. At least around Mother and Dinah, I felt disagreeable most all the time.

But at school I had a secret life. I might not have been the best student, but I did behave. My fifth-grade teacher wrote on my final report card, "It was a pleasure to have Addie in my class. She was a thoughtful and well-behaved presence all year."

Mother read it and said, "I can't believe this is you."

"It's not," I said. "She mixed me up with someone else."

Dinah and I had an invisible line down the middle of our room, and I did not go into enemy territory except to reach the door. Dinah's side of the room was neat as a pin. Mine was chaos. The mess on my half bothered Dinah more than it did me. In fact, it sometimes drove her nearly to hysterics, which I found reason enough to leave it that way. I cleaned my half of our room only under direct orders from Mother.

Mother got a secondhand car that year, which relieved us all, I believe. It was dented, and the driver's seat was torn, but it ran, and she drove it back and forth to work and shopping. And even I, who wished misfortune on Dinah, was glad not to see her struggling in the door after school with sacks of groceries.

In her last year of middle school Dinah was

made editor of the yearbook and elected president of the student council. Because of her position in the school, she often felt the need of new clothes for some occasion or another, and Mother strained her budget to provide them. There was no question: Dinah deserved them. She worked hard. She was worthy.

Which was why it was so odd that the miracle that happened that year happened to me.

It was on my twelfth birthday, a Monday, and I took my time on the way home from school as a treat to myself. I knew this was my last year to walk home through the canyon, because the middle school was in the opposite direction from home. If I was ever to see a deer, it would have to be soon.

The canyon was full of fresh green, the deer droppings were more numerous than ever, and I dawdled for maybe an hour that day, mostly sitting quietly on a rock. But in vain.

When I finally got home, Mother's car was already there in the drive. I was late, but she was early, and I was afraid at first that I'd get in trouble. But then I remembered it was my birthday, and Mother never got mad at any of us on her birthday. Never, ever. It was some sort of rule she had, and I liked it. A guaranteed day off.

Mother called to me the second I walked in the door.

"Addie, is that you?"

"Yes," I said.

"In here," she said, and I followed her voice to the living room.

And there it was. A miracle. Parked in the middle of the living-room floor. A shiny aquamarine mountain bike with hand brakes, ten gears, and reflectors in both wheels.

I gaped. I wanted it to be for me—and it *was* my birthday—but it was too much to hope for, really. It was too much to hope for, period. Mother didn't have money for gifts like this. Maybe it was for Dinah, and Mother was just showing it to me. It was a coincidence that she happened to be showing it to me on my birthday.

"It's beautiful," I said softly.

Mother didn't say anything.

I gathered all my courage and asked, "Who is it for?"

"For you," Mother said.

"Really?" I couldn't believe it. I simply could not believe that this gorgeous, gleaming bicycle was for me! I turned around to thank her. She was about to get the biggest thanks of her entire life!

But when I saw her expression, something stopped me. Her face was a neutral mask, and her arms were folded across her chest.

"It's from your father," she said. She did not smile.

Daddy. It's from . . . I walked over to the bike and carefully, gingerly, touched the seat. *Daddy.*

"How?" I said. "How did it get here?"

But nobody answered. Mother had left the room.

I did not know what to make of the bike. Partly I just couldn't get it through my head that it was really mine. I wanted it. Oh, how I wanted it! But I also expected it to disappear at any moment.

It's from your father. But how? Had he brought it himself? Was it delivered? No tag, no note, no carton. A mystery. I sniffed the air, trying to catch a scent of Daddy. Had he actually stood in this room? After nearly five years with no word from him, had he come to this house and gone without waiting to say hello?

It didn't make sense. If he cared this much—enough for this bike—then why did he never come see me? Why couldn't he at least call?

I stared at the spot where Mother had stood just moments before. I was suddenly certain she had the answers to all of my questions. Every one. And I was just as certain that if I asked, birthday or no, she'd make me sorry I had.

For you. For me.

This bike is mine. And then that was all that really mattered. Without my telling him, without my telling anybody, Daddy had somehow known my very heart's desire, and had provided.

I wheeled the bicycle to the front door and hollered, "I'm going out." Like that. No "May I?" *Today is my birthday and this is my bike and I'm going out.*

"You be careful," Mother called. "Be back in an hour."

"I will," I said.

You can travel so far on a bike. You can get there and back so quickly. I tasted a new freedom that day. The wind blew my hair back, and the sun bounced off the aquamarine frame, and ten gears were more than I'd need in a lifetime, but I used them all. I traveled the whole world over and returned in exactly one hour.

I imagine I had a cake that night, and that Mother and Dinah and the twins sang "Happy

Birthday." But I do not remember any of that. I only remember that I wheeled the bike into the garage and wiped it down with a soft rag, and that I knew it was there when I fell asleep.

Ten

There came a time when, no matter how I might have wished otherwise, I knew I no longer fit in. Not at home, not at school, not anywhere. Even among friends I felt vaguely out of place and in the wrong.

I wondered, for a while, if my clothes were at fault. They were all hand-me-downs from Dinah, and because of that were persistently three years out-of-date. But even as I wondered, I knew it was more serious than clothes. It was something about me.

In eighth grade I was friendly for a while with Elyse McKay, who wore her hair in a French braid even though no one else did and often came to school with a paisley scarf wrapped around her waist. She was lively and laughed a lot and didn't seem to notice that some kids thought she was weird. And I admired her for that. I wanted to be like her.

I rode my bike to her house one Saturday and was stunned to discover that Elyse's mother laughed and mussed her hair when Elyse said and did things I'd have been punished for. It made me anxious. So anxious I finally had to leave. I was convinced that at any moment her mother would explode from behind her veneer of friendliness and shed blood.

I had almost the same sensation when I spent the night with Robin Estrada. Her parents took us out for ice cream, gave us money to rent two movies, then seemed completely unconcerned when we burned the popcorn and had to open all the downstairs windows. I did not want to go back.

I decided I was a loner, and that maybe I'd been born that way and was only now noticing.

I experimented with my hair and clothes, and because by now I did not wish to look or be anything like Dinah, I altered her castoffs or shunned them altogether. I cut the cuffs off shirts and the collars off blouses. I wore a silver earring in one ear and traded Debbie Horowitz my digital watch for a gray flannel vest that I loved. The watch was a Christmas gift from Mother, which she had meant to help get me home on time, and I lied and said I'd lost it and endured the screaming fit that followed. The vest was worth it.

And I wore the black hat. It fit almost perfectly now, and I turned the brim down in front and wore it everywhere.

Mother said I looked a disgrace, and I said, "Now at least I look like what I am," and went to my room before she could order me there.

I was assigned to art class for the second semester of eighth grade. I already knew—had always known—that I couldn't draw my way out of a paper bag, and I was depressed at the thought of receiving a grade in a subject for which I had no talent whatsoever.

Our first assignment was a self-portrait, and Mr. Lemle, our teacher, was not moved when I raised my hand and said I absolutely, positively could not draw people. No how. No way.

"Just draw," he said. "Effort counts. Feeling counts. Skill does not count. Yet."

Effort. Feeling. I did not know how to make those things happen on a piece of paper. But I set to work.

I did the background first, because I felt more confident of that, and left a hole for the person who might come later. I drew desert mountains in the distance in tans and soft oranges and faint purples. In the middle ground I drew a post-and-barbed-wire fence with what I hoped looked like a coyote carcass hanging across it. I scattered a half-dozen sagebrushes of pale gray-green in the foreground. And I drew a tumbleweed, bleached by the sun and all rounded from bouncing along over the desert on its way to nowhere. I spent an entire class period on that tumbleweed, and it still didn't look real—which is why I hate to draw.

Then I went to work on me, Addie Dillon. I sketched in regular pencil first, drawing myself from the feet up—boots, jeans, a loose flowered blouse, the vest, and the black hat pulled so low over my face you could only see the mouth and chin. In my right hand I put Damnhorse's bridle. It sounds better than it was. It was not good.

I studied it for a time, then decided that one of the main things wrong was that there was entirely too much of me. So I took a ruler and drew a line right down the middle, and erased all of me to the right of the line. I filled in the space with background, then colored in the half of me that remained. Then I was satisfied.

And that's how I ended up in the counselor's office.

At first I didn't know why I was there. I'd never been called to the counselor's office before, and I nearly jumped out of my skin when my homeroom teacher hung up the intercom phone and said, "Adelaide Dillon, report to room 115."

Mrs. Phillips, the school counselor, was a middle-aged woman with short blond hair, thick glasses, and an expression that gave nothing away. She said, "Please sit down, Adelaide." And that's when I spotted my drawing on her desk.

"Do you prefer Adelaide or Addie?" she asked.

"Addie," I said. "Unless I'm in trouble. Then it's Adelaide. Am I in trouble?"

"I don't know," she said. "Are you?"

Somehow I thought she was supposed to know the answer to that, but since it wasn't decided yet, I said, "I can explain about that drawing."

"I wish you would," she said, and leaned back in her seat.

"I really can't draw at all," I said. Then I went on and told her how I'd started the picture and how I'd ended up. "If I could draw, maybe I'd have done it differently," I said. "So how much trouble am I in?"

Mrs. Phillips smiled. "None at all with me."

"With Mr. Lemle, then," I guessed.

"No," she said, "I don't think you're in trouble with Mr. Lemle either. He brought me your drawing because he thought it was interesting. He thought I might want to meet someone who drew half a person as a self-portrait."

"Huh," I said.

Mrs. Phillips sat quietly and looked at me for a bit. I felt she was studying me, and that made me uncomfortable, so when I couldn't stand the silence any longer, I said, "It's like me in a way."

"Is that how you feel, Addie? Like half a person?"

"In a way," I said. I didn't know it was true until I said it, but that was just how I felt. Like half of me wasn't there.

We both sat quietly for a while longer, and then, maybe because I couldn't think of anything to say, Mrs. Phillips said, "Tell me a little about your family, why don't you?"

I shrugged. "It's just a regular family," I said. Then I went ahead and told her about the twins who were now nine years old, and about Dinah who was president of the honor society at Adams High School, and how my parents were divorced and I didn't know where my father was, and how Mother was always worried about money, and how I knew it was hard to raise four children all by yourself.

"And that's why I really don't want detention," I said. "I already cause enough trouble, and Mother will slaughter me."

"You cause trouble?" Mrs. Phillips asked. She sounded doubtful.

"Constantly," I said.

"How?"

So I told her. "Because I don't really help and my room is a pigsty and my grades stink," I said. "I'm unmotivated."

Mrs. Phillips opened a folder on her desk and scanned through several papers. "Your grades don't look so bad to me," she said. "The only thing here lower than a C is math. You do seem to have trouble right along with math."

"And art," I said. "I'm zero in math and art."

"Well," she said. "I'm not so concerned about math and art right now. I'm much more interested in how much trouble you're in and who the trouble is with."

"My mother," I said. That was easy. "And Dinah. They're completely fed up with me. They have been for years. They think I'm going to end up in a gang, or pregnant, or on drugs."

Mrs. Phillips raised her eyebrows. "And are you?" she asked.

I felt a rush of anger for no reason that I could make out. I knew the answer to the question—had known it long before Mrs. Phillips ever asked—but I had to decide first whether I felt like telling anyone.

I stared out the window while I thought it over, then said, "No, I am not. I wouldn't give Mother and Dinah the satisfaction."

Mrs. Phillips fixed me with a piercing look. "Too stubborn, huh?" she said.

"I guess," I said.

Then the corners of her mouth ticked up in a wry smile. "Well, good for you," she said. "Keep it up."

She pulled a sheet of paper from a desk drawer, looked at the clock, and wrote, "Pass 9:25 A.M. T.L. Phillips." Then she handed it to me.

"Come back and see me, Addie."

"When?" I asked.

"Anytime you like," she said. "It's an invitation, not an order. Drop by anytime, so long as my door is open. I'll give you a pass."

"Well . . ." I said. "Okay. Maybe."

"I hope you do," she said. "I'd like to get to know you better."

As I rushed up the stairs toward my English class, I thought about whether I'd go back to see Mrs. Phillips. And then I noticed the time on the pass. It was now only 9:15. My school was strict with passes. Usually you had about one minute to get where you were going, and if you didn't make it, you got sent to the office—which might be where you came from in the first place. Evidently, Mrs. Phillips thought I could be trusted on the loose for ten minutes without torching the school.

I went to the girls' room and fooled with my hair. Maybe I would go back and see her sometime.

The next time I saw my drawing, Mr. Lemle was hanging it on the wall in the art room, along with about five others from my class. He gave it an A and wrote "Very expressive" on the back. I looked at the other drawings and knew mine wasn't anywhere near as good, so I was suspicious of the A. I hoped it wasn't a pity grade. I did not want that.

I made up my mind to ask Tiny and Bits when I got to take it home what they thought of the drawing. They would tell the truth. I could count on that from them, even if they made one of their dolls do the dirty work. Bowsie would say, "I regret to inform you, Addie, this drawing is hideous."

The twins were skinny nine-year-olds, all arms

and legs. Their once curly blond hair was now frizzy blond hair. It stuck out in all directions, giving them a wild, almost insane look that did not match the usual composure of their faces.

They lived almost apart from us, as though surrounded and protected by an invisible force field that could not be penetrated by evil. But they watched. They saw everything and they knew. And they always told the truth.

It was five weeks before my drawing came off the wall and I rolled it up to carry home and show to the twins.

What I was thinking about as I turned the corner onto Maybeck Road that afternoon was Mrs. Phillips. I'd been to see her about three different times, and it seemed I could tell her about just anything and she was always interested. I'd stopped in to see her that afternoon after math class, because we'd had a test that I was certain I'd flunked. But I ended up talking about Damnhorse instead of math, and then started crying when I realized Damnhorse might even be dead by now and turned into glue. If they do that with dead horses anymore. I don't know.

So with all of that on my mind, I didn't hear Tiny and Bits hollering until they were nearly on top of me. I saw them first, careening down the hill in the wagon with the sides off, and Bits was steering and Tiny was yelling, "Addie! Addie!" and I thought they were going to crash. Which they did, although they managed to slow down some first so it wasn't too bad.

I dropped my backpack and rushed to help them up, but Tiny was hollering, "Addie, go home! Run!"

And Bits yelled, "Run, Addie! Go now! Mama's doing something, and you have to hurry! *Run.*"

I wanted to stop and ask questions, but I could tell by the yelling and the horror on their faces that I'd better just run. So I did. All the way up the hill and around the bend and into the front yard, where I could see Marta's car in the driveway and Mother loading my bike into her trunk.

"What are you doing?" I yelled.

Mother whirled toward me, startled. Then her expression turned fierce. "Go in the house," she said.

"That's my bike. *What are you doing with my bike?*"

"Go in the house," she said again. Now she was angry.

"No!" I said. "Not until you tell me what you're doing with my bike!"

"I sold it," she said. "Now go."

"You can't do that. You can't! It's *my bike.*"

"I can and I did," Mother said. "You've been riding it recklessly, and it's time to get rid of it."

"That's not true!" I said. "I always ride carefully. Always!"

"Dinah saw you," she said.

"*It's a lie!*" I said. "You can't sell my bike because of some lie Dinah told. It's not fair."

"It's too late," Mother said. "Anyway, I needed the money. So get inside. Now!"

Marta, who'd been standing silently by, said, "You took good care of this bike, Addie. Lizzy will be pleased."

Lizzy. Mother was giving my bike to Lizzy!

I turned and ran in the house and slammed the

door, then leaned against it. My chest was pounding and my head roared.

You took good care of this bike. Of course I took good care of it. I loved that bike! I never once rode it without wiping it clean afterward. It had three coats of wax on the frame and fresh oil on the gears.

I went to the living-room window and watched as Mother and Marta jiggled the bike this way and that to make it fit in the trunk. They didn't even know how to load a bike. I just knew they were scratching it. Then Marta tied the trunk down with a rope.

Lizzy will be pleased. Like I'd been taking care of it for Lizzy! I didn't take care of it for Lizzy—I took care of it for *me.* Lizzy would ruin it!

I ran all the way upstairs and into my bedroom and slammed that door, too. Then I kicked it hard and left scuff marks all over it and was not sorry. Not sorry and not satisfied. I looked around for something. What? Then I spotted the silver-backed mirror on Dinah's dresser. Mother's pride and joy. Now Dinah's pride and joy. I picked it up and flung it with all my might against the far bedroom wall. It shattered on impact and fell to the floor in a shower of glass.

Then I sat down. I sat on my bed and just stared straight ahead and felt hatred. Pure hatred. Undiluted. I sat there for maybe half an hour, hating, and while I hated, something inside of me slowly turned to stone. I felt the change as it took place, and I remember asking myself, *I wonder if it's a good idea to turn to stone? Maybe I should try to stop.* But then I thought, *No, this is really for the best.*

Dinah came in, saw the mirror, shrieked, and ran out again. Straight to Mother, of course. Then Mother yelled for me to get right downstairs that very instant. I went, wondering what she could possibly do to me that mattered.

She slapped me right away, then screamed a lot, but I didn't really listen to what she was saying. I watched her face and the way her mouth changed shape around her teeth and wondered if her hand stung from the slap.

Then she was suddenly quiet, and I realized she was waiting for an answer. But what was the question? Oh, yes, something about what I had to say for myself.

"You had no right to sell my bike," I said. "My father gave it to me, and you had no right."

I guess she went berserk then, because she grabbed me by the shoulders and yelled some more, then shoved me up against the wall and shook me while my head banged against the plaster. Bang. Bang. Bang. Bang. Bang. And then the plaster cracked and I heard it. And some fell on the floor, and I heard that, too. And then she stopped.

"If you're done, I'd like to go back to my room," I said. I was woozy, but also determined not to show it.

Mother looked frightened. Of what? Of me? Of herself? But she didn't answer, so I left.

I found the twins sitting at the top of the staircase. Tiny had my backpack on her lap, and silent tears streamed down Bits's cheeks.

I reached for the backpack. "It's okay," I said to them. "Don't worry. She can't hurt me anymore. Nobody can hurt me now."

And it was true. *I feel absolutely nothing. I am made of stone.*

It was days before I thought of my drawing again, and by the time I did, it was long gone. I must have dropped it down the hill at the wagon wreck, and I guess it blew away.

But I knocked on the twins' door, anyway, to ask if they'd seen it, and Tiny opened the door—just a crack at first.

"Oh, it's you, Addie," she said. "You can come in."

What I remember of that moment is walking into their room and seeing a scene of utter carnage. The Barbie dolls were all dismembered. Torsos and limbs were scattered about, and the heads of two of them hung by their hair from the window shades. Even Tansy and Bowsie were feet up in the trash can.

"What are you *doing* to your dolls?" I asked.

"They were bad," Tiny said.

"We're punishing them," Bits said. "They have to be punished so they'll learn how to behave."

I don't know if it was the sight of the dolls, or the calm, almost cheerful way the twins spoke, but I backed out of the room then.

They're only dolls. I reminded myself of that. *After all, they're only dolls, and this is just pretend.* But something about it sent prickles down my spine.

Later I went for a long walk. Partly I wanted to take one last look for that drawing, but also I wanted to be out in the air. Without planning to, I ended up in the canyon. I hadn't been there since grade school, and there was something strangely comforting about going back. I walked down the trail to my favorite resting rock and sat there in the sunlight and wondered. I wondered about me, and how long I would be made out of stone. And I wondered about the twins, and whether it was such a good idea that they still played with dolls. And I wondered about all of us.

And then, while I was still wondering, I saw a deer.

Eleven

It's funny how I remember that deer, how I remember the glistening liquid brown of its eyes and then the flicking white of the underside of its tail as it bounded lightly up the hillside. That deer is as sharp and clear in my memory as if I'd seen it yesterday, when so much that follows is dim . . . or gone entirely.

I slept. And slept, and slept, and slept. Through most of my freshman year at Adams High School, I fought a daily battle just to keep my eyes open. One grim day in Biology I stuck the point of a mechanical pencil into one palm and held it there, pushing with just enough pressure to keep me in painful consciousness. But at home I lost every battle. Even on days when I came home bound and determined to dive right into my homework, my eyes drifted shut within minutes. I could not stay awake. I'd give up and crawl into bed and sleep soundly until someone—Dinah or one of the twins—woke me for dinner. And then I'd conk out again before ten o'clock. I was drowning in sleep, and I do not know why.

Dinah said I was just terminally lazy, and maybe she was right. But Mother decided there was something suspicious about a daughter who nodded off at odd times and one day searched my room. "Tossed" it, I think they say in the movies—although she didn't do such a good job, because she never did find those photos and the Wellington Motors pen. But when she was done, all flushed in the face from the effort and maybe frustrated, too, she put her hands on her hips and demanded to know if I was taking drugs.

I guess I could have saved us both some trouble if I'd denied it right off, but I was mad by then and not feeling cooperative, so I did not answer. Just stared at her until she turned on her heels and left the room. Then the very next day she was waiting for me when I got home from school, and hauled me off to old Dr. Wexler, who never mentioned sleep or drugs or any of it, but prodded and peered and ordered liquid samples from my body and sent me off with a handshake instead of the usual balloon. I suppose at fifteen I was too old for balloons. But I was somehow disappointed.

Mother didn't mention drugs again, or the results of any tests the lab might have done, but I decided I wasn't diseased or she would have told me so. After that I was left alone to sleep on, undisturbed. Which I did, on into the middle of sophomore year, when Maxwell J. Walker woke me up.

I still shudder that I chose English class as the place to finally embarrass myself by dozing off in school. It was my favorite class that year, and Miss Gould was my favorite teacher. And Max, who sat in the seat in front of mine in the row along the wall, was the last person I would have wanted to think I was some kind of flake.

Half the girls in the school adored him. Half of *every*body in the school adored him. And maybe the only person in Adams High School who wouldn't have been impressed by that was Max himself. He didn't belong to any special crowd, and he wasn't cool like the boys who always had the ultimate shoes. Max was just Max. His two front teeth overlapped slightly, and his ears were larger than absolutely necessary, and he smiled a lot, so you noticed the teeth and the way his ears hiked up a little with each grin. Then you smiled back, whether you meant to or not.

It was only later that you might notice there was something special about his eyes, and that he was really almost handsome in his own, personal, Max Walker kind of way.

There were times in English class when Max clowned and caused a disruption. Then there were other times. Like when he read T. S. Eliot aloud with such feeling it left me breathless, and the stillness in the class was so complete you'd have heard a pin drop. Miss Gould—tough, no-nonsense Miss Gould—was sold on Max. So, for that matter, was I.

So that's why I'd rather have been anywhere else on that day late in January when, sitting sideways in my seat, I propped my chin in my hand and leaned gently against the bulletin board.

The next thing I knew, Max was tapping on my head with a pen. "Miss Gould has her eye on you," he said. "I think she's going to ask you to read Poe."

I snapped alert and rifled frantically through the

pages of our poetry book. Poe. I didn't even know what chapter he was in. How could I doze off in Miss Gould's class? What would she think? And Max Walker! Only an airhead would fall asleep in class.

I looked up and found Max watching me. His eyes were dancing. That's when I first understood what it was about his eyes—they danced. I flipped to the index of the book and ran my finger down to the *P*s. Max slid a folded sheet of paper onto my desk. I opened it, expecting it to give the page number for the Poe. Instead, it read, *You drool when you sleep.*

I looked up at him again and his eyes were still dancing, only now they were laughing, too. In fact, his whole face was laughing, though he didn't make a sound, and I blushed, furiously uncontrollably. Because I *had* drooled. My chin was still damp.

And that's how Max and I became friends.

For a long time, our entire friendship consisted of Max teasing me about sleeping in class, and of me blushing. No matter how I swore not to, I blushed every time. Next, he acted as though the reason for my condition had to do with my social life, as though I were out late every night! I blushed even more then, partly because his guess was so far from the truth. The only boy who had ever asked me out was a freshman named Stevie Underwood, and Mother had made it clear I would be old enough to date when I was a senior, *if* I had demonstrated a sense of responsibility by then.

But Max didn't know that. I think he only knew he had a surefire way to make me turn beet red in the middle of e. e. cummings, and he slipped me notes every day, brazenly, right in front of Miss Gould:

Late night again?

Who is he?

If he's left-handed, don't trust him!

I hope he's not the kind of guy who wears cologne.

I didn't answer the notes. Not because they were dopey, which they were. But because I was too busy blushing and fumbling. And anyhow I didn't dare; I was not teacher's pet. So I folded each note, stuck it in a notebook, and took it home and kept it. A relic.

Soon Max was on my mind almost every minute of the day, and I was no longer sleepy. I began to wish my clothes weren't so original. Or that they were *more* original. Or even alluring. Anything that might cause Max to stop thinking of me as I imagined he must—as a complete moron. Each morning I tried on clothes in different combinations. Then, on the way to school, I tried on sentences. Today I would say something smooth, clever, something . . . arresting.

But I lost confidence in both clothes and speech before I ever got to English class, and sat there day after day tongue-tied. I mentally answered Max's notes as though my phantom boyfriend were real. *No, Max, he's not left-handed like you, and he doesn't smell of fresh, woody soap, and he's not daring and bold and funny like you. And his eyes don't dance.*

In time—maybe because he'd run his joke into the ground—Max gradually teased me less. And then one day, when Miss Gould was late to class, he pulled out a deck of cards and started shuffling.

"Old Maid?" I said. "You must be kidding." Those were almost the first plain words I'd ever spoken to him.

"Bet you think it's childish," he said, and quickly dealt the cards between us. "But looked at another way, you could say Old Maid is deeply rooted in the symbolism of our age."

Then, while I was trying to work out whether he meant that seriously, and sort my cards into pairs at the same time, he said, "Mostly, though, it's childish. Which is the whole point. Now draw."

I laughed and instantly drew the Old Maid, then spent the next five minutes trying to get rid of it until Miss Gould arrived.

As spring came on, Max stopped by my locker some mornings to talk, and a couple of times we sat together at lunch. But mostly I remember hectic games of Old Maid in the three or four minutes before English started each day. Max got so he'd bring the deck in preshuffled and predealt, and slap my hand down on my desk as he walked past. He said he shuffled them at the end of Algebra class each day. I was supposed to trust him, and I did.

We played ferociously, goading and bluffing, and hurrying each other, because part of the point was to finish the hand before Miss Gould got to class, but also hoping to rush the other into error. It was sudden death; whoever had the Old Maid when Miss Gould walked in lost.

"Come on, draw! Oh, yeah, take that one."

"Ha! It's a match. Thought you'd scare me off, right?"

"No, no, no. Hands off, that's my favorite card! Gotcha! It's the Old Maid."

Then one day, when Max was stuck with the Old Maid at the end of an eight-day losing streak, he put the card to his mouth and ripped it to shreds with his teeth. I guess it took me by surprise, because suddenly I was howling with laughter. Tears rolled and my sides ached, and if Miss Gould hadn't given me several threatening looks I don't know how I'd have stopped. Then, over the next few minutes, I erupted over and over again in unwanted giggles. It was awful—I had completely lost it.

Maybe a quarter of an hour later, when I'd finally collected myself, a piece of the Old Maid card came flying over Max's shoulder and landed on my desk, and I started up again.

This time Miss Gould said sharply, "Addie!" She meant business.

I wrote Max a note. *Don't you dare get me thrown out of this class! I'll kill you, I swear.* I'd never been thrown out of a class in my life, and I didn't intend to start now.

He kept the note awhile, then returned it with a note of his own. *Will you go to the Spring Casual with me?*

Blink. Would I! I grabbed my pen, scrawled YES! And handed the paper back. Yes, I'd go to the dance with Max! I'd go to the moon with him if he asked.

For the rest of the day I walked in a fog. Not sleepy—I hadn't been sleepy for weeks. Just delerious, dazed.

Now I wonder who I thought I was. Someone who could just say yes to a dance and didn't need permission? I was on my way home before I remembered about Mother and my heart sank. She'd never allow me to go.

But . . . maybe. If I caught her in just the right mood, asked her in an offhand way. Maybe she'd say yes. She might give me permission without really thinking about it, almost by accident really. That could happen.

For two days I was watchful and carefully well behaved. Then, while she was drinking coffee and smiling over something in the Sunday paper, I made my move.

"Absolutely not," she said. "I don't like what I've heard about what goes on at those dances. They're very poorly chaperoned." Whatever good mood she'd been in had vanished in an instant.

"Teachers are there," I said. "And what goes on is *dancing*. It's just a dance, Mother."

"That's not what I heard from Dinah," she said.

"But Dinah went. You let her go."

"Dinah's different," Mother said. "Dinah has always—"

"Stop!" I said. "I don't want to hear how responsible and mature Dinah is. If you won't let me go, then fine. But please, don't tell me any more about Dinah. I don't want to hear it!" I turned and ran up to my room.

The oddest thing is that I wasn't even very angry or upset with Mother for turning me down. Maybe I had known all along she'd never give me permission to go to that dance.

But maybe I also knew all along that I was going anyway. It wasn't even something I decided, at least not as far as I know. It was just something that *was*. I was going to that dance. I'd be a liar and a sneak, but I would go.

When Max asked a few days later about coming to pick me up, I said it would be best if I just met him at the dance . . . because my mother wasn't feeling very well. Which I decided was a form of the truth. And then I made the rest of my plans very carefully. I picked my clothes and got them ready and hanging in my closet early in the week, so I wouldn't be noticed making preparations. And I figured that if I raced right home from school on the day of the dance, I could shower and have my hair dried before Mother even got there. For the rest I'd cross my fingers. And I did, every day.

But by the Friday of the dance I was a wreck. Deceit was far more worrying than I'd counted on. And then there was the rain. A late spring storm had blown in overnight, the kind you can sometimes get just when you've given up hope of ever seeing rain again before fall—one last good soaking for the earth before it baked under cloudless summer skies. Only now I did not want it. As the day passed, I watched the sky from classroom windows, hoping to see a break. If it didn't stop, I'd arrive at the dance a sodden mess. But the rain came in wind-driven gusts and torrents all day and was still falling when I left school.

I reached home wet and worried, and a shower, even a warm one, was the last thing I wanted. More water. But I headed for the family room to collect clean towels from the couch.

Tiny and Bits were in there, huddled at the window watching the storm.

"It's lousy out, isn't it?" I said.

"Oh, Addie, come look at the lilac bush," Bits said. "It's going to be ruined!"

"We have to do something!" Tiny said. "Addie, it's going to die."

I went and stood beside them. Our late-blooming lilac, heavy with blossoms, was bent nearly to the ground, almost touching the very spot where Lord Rodhopper had once been buried. Every so often a gust of wind whipped it up and back and nearly over in the other direction.

"It's taking a beating," I said, "but I don't think it'll die. Don't worry, really. Plants are strong. I think it will be okay. And some things you can't do anything about, like the weather."

"But we have to help," Tiny said.

"You can't," I said. "But you don't have to watch either. Just come away from the window and don't look. It will be okay."

They backed away from the window a couple of feet but didn't take their eyes off the lilac. I stood and watched them a minute, feeling helpless myself, then went for the towels.

The next thing I knew, Bits was in the kitchen, rummaging frantically through the utensil drawer. She came up with the poultry shears and bolted for the back door. Tiny was right with her. I don't think a word had passed between them.

I watched out the window as Bits snipped off lilac blossoms and dropped them into the basket of Tiny's skirt. The rain lashed, and Bits struggled time after time to catch the blowing lilac branches in her hand. I knew better than to try to stop them, and they didn't need my help, but I stood at the window, unable to take my eyes off the twins, as they stripped the blossoms from the tree. When every blossom had been cut, the lilac bush stood nearly straight again.

They came back in then, soaked absolutely to the skin. Their hair hung heavy and matted, and their dresses clung to their thin shoulders. They looked at me, then at each other, and suddenly they were stricken and weeping.

"What?" I asked. "What is it? What's wrong?"

"We only wanted to help," Tiny said, gulping. "We wanted to rescue the blossoms so the tree wouldn't break."

"And you did," I said. "You were right—they were too heavy in the rain."

"But suppose . . ." Bits said, "suppose they didn't *want* to be rescued. Suppose the blossoms are going to be lonely now. Oh, Addie, I'm afraid these blossoms are very unhappy!" And then she sobbed.

I don't know what I said, but I said something. Words meant to soothe and console, to let them know they'd done the right thing and saved both the blossoms and the bush. But they didn't hear me or weren't convinced. They continued weeping, though more softly, as they got two buckets, filled them with water, and carefully set the lilac blooms inside.

I left them then and went upstairs to shower. I had a dance to get ready for. But the scent of lilacs followed me up the stairs. Something had happened, I felt. Something more than the storm and the cutting of lilac blossoms. Whatever it was—if it was anything at all—I knew that the twins understood it and I didn't.

That night we ate in silence. A great bouquet of lilacs overflowed from a vase in the center of the table, and masses more still sat in buckets on the kitchen sink, filling the air with an almost overpowering scent. Outside, the storm had finally died, and the twins sat, pale, their eyes rimmed in red, picking at their food. I concentrated most of my efforts on behaving absolutely normally. Whatever that was. No fidgeting, nothing to give away excitement or fear. I didn't dare speak, but my heart raced, and I wondered if I looked as posed and artificial as I felt. If anyone had dropped a fork, I'd have jumped from my skin.

I cleared and stacked the dishes with the twins—they were washing that night—and finally went to my room. For minutes I sat still, listening, anxious. Then I dressed quickly, brushed and fluffed my hair, and put on makeup with shaking hands. Too much. I grabbed a tissue and rubbed it mostly off. I listened at the door. Escape depended on Mother going to her room. I'd never get past her if she stayed downstairs.

I paced and watched the clock and listened. Twenty minutes passed, then forty. I was going to be late. Then, at last, I heard her go into her room to take a phone call. Freedom. I grabbed my purse and jacket, turned out the light, tiptoed quickly down the stairs, then headed for the back door, the quiet door.

Tiny and Bits were at the kitchen sink, sorting lilacs into every vase we owned. They saw me, of course, and gaped.

"Don't ask," I said. "If you ask, you might have to tell. . . ."

"We *wouldn't,*" Bits said, hurt.

"I know," I said quickly. I knew they wouldn't tell. They'd die first. "I only mean you'd have to lie. It's better if you don't know."

"You look nice, though," Tiny said.

"Thanks," I said. I moved toward the door.

"Wait!" Bits said. She brought a sprig of lilac and stuck it in the barrette on one side of my hair.

"I'm late," I whispered.

"Just a second more, Addie—you don't want it to fall out. Ah . . . there. Oh, it's beautiful. And now you'll smell like lilac." Bits stood back and beamed. It was the first smile I'd seen in hours.

I patted the blossom. "Is it really okay?" I asked.

"It's perfect," Tiny said.

"Thanks, you two." I gave them each a squeeze, then silently went out the door.

I remember that dance not by music, but by the scent of lilac that followed me all night. And by the lights that swirled around us, fragments of changing color. They left me with shards of memory, all smells and textures and colors mixed together, like pieces of a gemlit dream. First, with bright ruby reds billowing around us, there was Max's delighted laugh. I had just found him and confessed that up to now I'd only ever square danced. Who had laughed at me like that before? Someone. Owen? My father? I don't recall.

Later, standing in a flash of cold, harsh whites, like diamonds, Max said this night would have to do instead of the senior prom, because his family was moving to Seattle over the summer. His father's business had transferred him. Max was leaving. He couldn't! The white moved in a dizzying kaleidoscope until he said, "Don't be upset, Addie. We still have time. A month or two. We can go places. . . ." And I made myself forget.

And still later, when Max folded his arms

around me in a slow dance, and kissed me, soft, just in front of my ear, bits of deep sapphire blue floated in the air. The light warmed on my skin and then raced through me, tinkling and bright, and I felt what it was to glow.

In the colored light we danced and laughed and talked, and sometimes said nothing at all. And then, because once upon a time someone had made a mistake, and created a world in which dances had to end, it was over.

Max and I wandered hand in hand through the crowd and out into the cool night air. I was drifting, content, and Max was saying something . . . what? . . . when I saw it. At the curb. A familiar battered green automobile, jolting me from my dream.

I turned away, then back again. It was still there. I stood paralyzed as the driver's door opened and someone stepped out. My mother's voice pierced across thirty feet of lawn, "Adelaide Dillon! Get in this car!"

So Max was wrong about time. We had no more time, none at all. Mother blamed him as well as me for my sneaking out, although I told her it was all my doing. Not that I think it would have mattered if she'd believed me. I had behaved as she'd always known I would. Which I think is how she knew. She'd been waiting for me to do something like that—had waited for years. So when the moment came, she was ready. Worse, I was not sorry. I never regretted going to that dance. What I did regret was getting caught. I was not allowed to see Max outside of school again.

On the last day of school he gave me a pack of

Old Maid, gift wrapped. Then, in midsummer, when all of California was dry and cracked and shimmering in golden heat, he phoned to say good-bye.

I put the cards and all of Max's notes, and that sprig of lilac, pressed and faded in waxed paper, safely into hiding under the bureau drawer. That was two years ago, and they're still there. If I open the waxed paper, a faint whiff of lilac escapes, and I can see the colored lights again . . . although not Max.

I haven't played Old Maid again. Not yet. But maybe, when I'm older, I'll meet another boy. And maybe I'll be grown by then. And maybe, if I'm lucky, his eyes will dance.

Twelve

Dear Addie—Thank you so much for the money, which I will use for something you'd approve of—like to rent ice skates. There's a pond near campus, and I used the last money you sent to go skating with a bunch of kids from my dorm—at night! It was incredible! I don't believe anyone earns as much as you claim you do baby-sitting, but you're right, by the time I'm done buying toothpaste and doing the laundry, I never have enough left for anything fun. So you see what a difference you make.

Christy had her little sister up from Boston last weekend, and she camped out in our room in a sleeping bag on the floor. Sarah (her sister) is your age, and she and Christy enjoy each other so much, it got me to thinking about you. We used to be such good friends—do you remember that, Addie? Do you remember the games of hide-and-seek we used to play when we were little? I'll never forget the time you hid in the hamper—which was brilliant because I never would have found you in a million years—but there was something mildewed in there and when you got out, you stank! We laughed so hard. Remember how we sat at the dinner table that night and Mama kept saying, "What is that awful smell?"

And the plays we put on. Of course, I always took the part of the heroine, but you got so into your parts! You were probably the best Rumpelstiltskin in the history of the universe, even though you complained the whole time about how I always made you play the bad guy. It's funny—I actually admired the way you threw yourself into the things that I didn't want to do. Like the way you got up on Damnhorse when I wouldn't. Do you remember?

What happened to us, Addie? Why did we stop being friends? It seems like such a waste, somehow. And now we're three thousand miles apart, and even though we don't fight anymore, when I do come home we hardly talk. We write each other polite letters. Don't misunderstand me—I'm glad to get your letters. But I wish we knew each other a little better. It's odd how I remember you, while at the same time I don't think I really know you anymore. Who are you, Addie? I'd like to know that.

I guess what I'm trying to say is that I feel like we lost something special a long, long time ago, and I want it back. I miss you.

I'm sitting here writing to you because I want to, but I also need to write to Mother, and I'm dreading that. I've realized I don't want to go to medical school, and she's going to be terribly disappointed because she was counting on it. But how can I become a doctor when I can't stand the sight of blood? I went on a tour of Tufts University Medical School, and when we got to the cadaver room I actually passed out. It was horrible. So I don't know what I want to do with my life, but I know it's not that. I'm afraid Mother is going to stop speaking to me or something, after all her years of hard work and sacrifice and hope. But I just can't live my life only to make her happy. I have the idea you'll understand this. I'm just not sure she will.

Okay, I have to go now. I hope you'll write to me and tell me what's going on with you, what you're thinking and feeling. I know I have you for a sister, but I want you for a friend.

Love,
Dinah

Thirteen

I'm going on seventeen now, and I'm in the room I used to share with Dinah, half of which is not as neat as it used to be, and the other half of which is not as messy as it used to be. I *should* be studying for a history exam, but I'm not. So I'm still the same—irresponsible.

The house is semi-quiet. Tiny and Bits are downstairs watching something on the family-room TV, and every so often I hear them laugh, so maybe it's a comedy. But with the twins, there's no telling.

And Mother is out, on a date, no less. She started dating this man shortly after Dinah went away to college, and I think he's kind of a stuffed shirt, but Mother seems happier, or less *un*happy, since she's been seeing him, and for that I'm thankful. I think she really misses Dinah, although she doesn't come right out and say so. She talks about her a lot, and frets about whether she has enough warm clothes for the eastern climate, and generally bursts with pride over her. But mostly Mother is so busy with work and with Bill—that's his name, Bill—that she doesn't have a lot of attention left over for anyone. Which may be just as well.

She's never hit me again since the day she sold my bicycle (or the day of the wagon wreck, which is how I prefer to think of it), and once in a while I can tell she's making a real effort to be nice to me. But, let's face it, I'm still a disappointment in most of the ways that matter to Mother, and I find myself backing away when she's friendly. It's not that I mistrust her, but there's one of us I don't exactly trust either—if that makes any sense. And, too, I got along without her for so long. . . .

We all had a scare last year. Owen got terribly sick with something called Hodgkin's disease, which can kill you, and we worried about him for months. I'd like to claim I worried more than anyone else, but the truth is that Owen is special to all of us, each in a different way. He's just a special person. Now the doctors say he's okay, but it's taking me awhile to get over the habit of thinking he'll one day up and vanish. I would hate that. Even if I don't see him often, it means something to me to know he's right there in Turlock where I can find him if ever I need to.

The main thing that's keeping me from studying for my exam—besides a complete lack of interest in history, that is—is a letter I got from Dinah the other day. It's sitting on my dresser right now, and I've read it about a dozen times and even started to answer it, except I'm not done. She asked me some hard questions—things I'm sure I must know the answers to. I'm just having some trouble putting them into words.

Like who am I, really? The more I think about

it, the more I realize I just don't know. I guess I've spent so much time worrying that I was on the verge of going bad, and wondering how to avoid it, that I never stopped to think what I'd do if that didn't happen. And now I wonder, shouldn't it have happened already—if it were going to at all, that is? So maybe I should make another plan for Addie Dillon, failed gangster.

Which means I'll need to figure out some things I'm good at. Right now, I only know some things I like. I like sunlight and wide, open spaces, and the wind in my hair, and anything wild and free. And maybe that's who I really am. It's a start anyway. I think I'll tell that to Dinah.

I remember the days when Dinah used to scratch me to sleep with a story, and there's another thing I want to tell her when I do send that letter—which is that I was afraid of Damnhorse at first, too. I think she should know that. She wasn't the only one.

I wear the black hat only on special occasions now. But I do still think about Daddy. And I still miss him. You'd think you'd get over missing someone after so many years, but I haven't. And sometimes I wonder if I ever will.

I'd like to see him again someday. And every time I think that, I start thinking about what I'll say to him if ever I do. First, I guess, I'm going to have to tell him how awfully mad I am that he went off and left me that way—just disappeared, and left me here with all this pointless hope and wondering. And then, when I'm done being mad, which may take awhile, I'll say all the things I would have said on the day of that last boat trip if I'd known I would never lay eyes on him again, which I didn't. Like that I love him. And that I'm grateful, really, for the way he always treated me as if I was a person who could *do* things, like someone who was able. And then, finally, I'll thank him for that bike. I really, really want to thank him for that bike.

I imagine him, always, somewhere in Nevada. Sometimes, in my mind, he is driving over a dirt road in a four-wheel drive, and the radio is on, and Randy Travis is singing,

> *I'm gonna love you forever,*
> *Forever and ever, amen.*

I can see Daddy, then. He's tapping the steering wheel and humming along with the radio, and squinting into the sunlight, waiting to catch sight of his sheep.

Then other times I can't picture my father at all. And that's when I think most of tumbleweeds. I see one drifting lightly over the desert floor on its way to somewhere . . . but where?

That's the mystery about tumbleweeds. What becomes of them? Sometimes you see a bunch pushed hard against a barbed-wire fence, all tangled and caught fast. But what about the rest, all those other tumbleweeds that are just out there, blowing around alone? Where are they going? Where do they end up?

I've thought about this a lot, and here's what I've decided: I think they're going home. Every single time I imagine a tumbleweed, I say to myself, *There's a tumbleweed going home.*

NATALIE HONEYCUTT is the author of several novels for younger readers, including *Invisible Lissa, The All New Jonah Twist,* and *Juliet Fisher and the Foolproof Plan.* The mother of two, she lives in McCloud, California.